DEUCE

A TENNYSON BEND NOVEL

PT AMBLER

Warning

Intended for an 18+ audience only. This book contains material that is intended for a mature, adult audience. It contains graphic language, explicit sexual content, and adult situations.

A TENNYSON BEND NOVEL

PT AMBLER

DEUCE

Burdened by family expectations, Spencer has fought long and hard on the pro-tennis circuit. He won't let anything mess with his winning streak. Especially if it risks his chance at an Australian Open wildcard entry. It should have been easy for him to forget an anonymous, locker-room hook up, but how's he supposed to do that when the same hot-as-hell guy shows up on centre court shouting "foot fault!" every time he serves?

Sidelined by a freak accident, Garrett will jump at any opportunity to referee again—no matter the sport. The second he recognises Spencer on centre court, the line between personal and professional blurs and he realises he's kissed his way into a serious conflict of interest. A fling is the last thing on his mind. Especially if it threatens his professional reputation. But there's something undeniable about Spencer that keeps him coming back for more.

The rules are clear. Intimacy between players and officials is strictly forbidden. Whatever their game plan, Spencer and Garrett must play it soon, because the tennis world is small, and secrets have a way of getting out...

AUTHOR'S NOTE

Special thanks go to the folks at the Tennis Australia Officials Team who, pre-global craziness, tried to teach me the intricacies of line umpiring.

Being the dreamer I am, my ability to focus on the line wasn't quite up to scratch, but I sure did learn a lot...*and* it sparked the first delicious ideas for *Deuce*.

I've played tennis since I stood barely the height of a racquet—so I know the game pretty well, but I took a lot of creative liberties in depicting the structure and management of a pro-tennis tournament. All mistakes are my own.

To keep this novel authentic to its Aussie roots, the author has used Australian English spelling and grammar.

Enjoy :)

CHAPTER ONE

Garrett

Garrett gritted his teeth and fought not to hold his breath. Every muscle shuddered with effort and a rivulet of sweat coursed down his spine.

"Push it. Push it. Aaaa-nd time." Kevin, his bastard of a physio, clicked his stopwatch. "Thirty seconds. Good job, G."

"Ugh." Garrett grunted with pain.

Not the bad kind of pain. That felt different.

It wasn't the sharp pain of a pinched nerve, or the fiery pain of tearing muscle, or the gut-wrenching pain of shattered bone.

No.

Nothing special.

The sort of pain that wracked Garrett's body was simple, garden-variety pain caused by scarred muscle and bone and tendons and ligaments all pushed to their limits.

For a long, agonising moment, Garrett was stuck in the squat. His thighs trembled, and he knew that if he didn't pull out of it soon, he'd either fall flat on his face or flat on his arse.

Since neither of those options were optimal, Garrett did his best to ignore the far-too-familiar strain. He clenched his teeth, held his breath, and squeezed his glutes together so hard he could probably have cracked a nut.

Gradually, trembling, sweating profusely, he pushed to stand.

The world spun, and his lungs forced him to haul in a jagged breath. "Ugh!"

"Whoa!" Kevin braced him from behind with a hand on either side of his waist, and Garrett grabbed for the wooden ballet barre attached to the mirrored wall beside him.

As Kevin's hands left him, Garrett turned to grip the wooden rod tight with both hands, then carefully shifted his full weight onto one leg, then the other, to shake them out. "You're evil. You know that, right?"

Reflected in the mirror, Kevin brought his hands together as though to pray and smiled an annoyingly happy smile, "Only on my good days."

"Grr." Garrett could've throttled him. Except if he did that, he'd be up the creek without a physio, and Kevin was the best in the business. Without his help, Garrett would probably still be hobbling on crutches. Maybe even in a wheelchair. "So, when's my next torture session?" he half-joked.

Please say never.

"Your strength and balance are recovering well, but we need to add a smidge more cardio to your regimen to work on your stamina. Keep that up, and I'll see you in a week. Ten days at most."

And if I don't? Garrett wanted to ask, but he didn't. Kevin was the kindest hard-arse that ever there was. If Garrett didn't do his exercises, Kevin would just smother him with more intense care.

No pain, no gain...right?

Well, he had the pain. One day soon, he hoped, the universe would deliver the gain.

"Hop up on the massage table, and I'll give you a rub down. Don't want you getting stiff on my watch," Kevin said.

"Wouldn't want that," he playfully smirked between groans as he hobbled across the floating wooden floors of the re-purposed ballet studio. Garrett knew his physio was oblivious to the innuendo—Kevin didn't have a gay bone in his body—but since Garrett's sex life had gone the way of the dodo the day of his accident, he couldn't pass up the opportunity to have a little fun. He parted the jewel-bead curtain hung in the doorway to the tiny side room set up for massage, and gratefully rolled, face first, onto the ancient leather massage table.

As far as gains went, a massage was fairly minor, but Garrett had learned to take what he could.

By the time he survived Kevin's final ministrations, and the forty-minute tram ride home from funky Carlton in Melbourne's north east, to his apartment in the rehabbed Docklands district in the south-west corner of the city, Garrett was beyond ready to chill.

"Ugh, you bastard!" Garrett finally managed to wrench open the door to his modern, utilitarian apartment.

The key worked fine.

As did the lock.

The problem was his body.

He dumped his stuff at the door, grabbed a beer from the fridge, eased his way down onto his soft-as-hell sofa, flicked on the television, and settled in for a few hours of whatever sport was going. He clicked through a few channels. It wasn't footy season, but beggars couldn't be choosers. Cricket would have to do.

Just as he raised his beer for another relieving gulp, his phone rang.

The jaunty sound was like barbed wire to his raw nerves. He winced as he reached over his head to the small side table.

Unknown number.

Garrett thought about not answering.

Not answering meant nobody could ask him stupid questions. Questions like, "You doing okay, mate? Feeling good? Raring to go?"

On a good day, his answer was, "No."

On a bad day, his answer was, "Hell, no."

But they amounted to the same thing.

No, he wasn't doing okay.

No, he wasn't feeling good.

No, he wasn't raring to go.

Maybe he never would be.

After the torture Kevin had put him through, every muscle and bone creaked, but he did his best to hold the groan in as he levered his torso off the leather sofa and sat up. Nobody told him having half his bones replaced with metal would make him feel like the fucking tin man—rusting from the inside out.

He swiped up on the green phone icon, because even though his answer was certain, admitting to the status quo would be worse.

"Hello," he answered, flatly.

"Hey, Garrett."

It took a second for Garrett's memory to catch up to the sound of his ex's voice.

"Jesus, Toby? Is that you?"

"Yeah. Hey. How're you doing?"

Garrett let that question shuttle away.

The last time Garrett had seen the man, Toby had belittled his choice of career. He'd called Garrett a cop-out for giving up his place at university and a career in sports psychology to go run around after a bunch of guys in short shorts on a footy field. It hadn't been too difficult to shut the door on the man's face.

Literally.

Probably figuratively too, but he wasn't so into words and grammar and whatever the fuck else his English teachers had tried to teach him back in school. They weren't his forte. His world was sports—physical accuracy; rules and regulations; keeping the score.

Well, it *was*—he'd not been doing much refereeing for the past few months from his sofa, or from his hospital bed before that.

Hearing Toby's voice again brought back all that he could no longer be. Which wasn't exactly Toby's fault.

In Toby's world, decisions weren't a matter of in or out, win or loss. Too much of a diplomat for black and white, he could fit an essay between yes and no. The last Garrett had heard, Toby had spurned the sports field and climbed the ladder into sports management—where everything was a fucking grey area.

Garrett didn't operate like that. Not if he could help it. He preferred to keep things simple. They'd fooled around some, back in the day, but when Toby decided he had a right to an opinion on Garrett's choices in life, Garrett had cut him loose.

Friends? Sure.

Casual fuck? If you like.

Relationship? Hell, no.

Not when he knew it wouldn't be forever.

It wasn't in Garrett to lie about his feelings. He'd seen the destructive power of that first-hand the day his mum went to the store for milk, with a suitcase in tow, and never came back. Garrett knew that when he eventually did fall for someone, and chose to commit, it wouldn't be for convenience, or because he felt some half-baked attraction. He wouldn't lie about his feelings, then up and disappear. When Garrett promised forever, he'd mean it. All or nothing.

Garrett's attention gravitated back to the cricket test on the screen. It was the fifth and last session of the Boxing Day Ashes test and the Aussies were in for a fight. If he hadn't been uncomfortable holding himself up for hours on end, he'd have been hovering on the edge of his seat—hanging over every cricket ball bowled.

Not that cricket was his game.

It might be played on the same oval field, but it wasn't footy. Not by a long shot.

Garrett fingered the mute on the remote, then warily tuned back in to Toby. He didn't hold any animosity toward Toby anymore, but the last thing he felt like doing was getting into a 'how ya doing' catch up with his ex. "What's up?" he asked.

"Yeah, so," Toby cleared his throat. "I heard you might be up for a job."

Hope made Garrett's heart trip. A job?

"You want me on the field?" Garrett couldn't keep the neediness from his voice.

Could they really want him to return?

Just the thought of being back out there on the footy ground, making calls. Hell, he'd even agree to stand stock still between the goal posts and wave a fucking flag if it meant being a referee again.

Except he'd not met the fitness requirements. He could barely jog twenty steps, let alone the twenty kilometres a referee needed to be able to run over the course of a professional game...and, the league doctors told him he probably never would.

Too much of a risk, they said.

Too much of a liability.

And the door had shut on his AFL refereeing career.

So, how was Toby now offering him a job?

"In a manner of speaking," Toby answered.

Garrett waited. He was already in his own quagmire. He wasn't about to wade into one of Toby's bullshit grey areas, too.

"Not footy," Toby said with uncharacteristic bluntness.

"Not footy?" *What else is there?*

They'd been doing the same sports psych Master's degrees, and met while hanging over adjacent blocks of a pool, officiating at the national swimming trials for the Rio Olympics. That was back when the certification hours required for their degrees meant they'd both grabbed for any volunteer offi-ciating role available—basketball, soccer, swimming. Hell, they'd even signed up together to ref for a lawn bowls tour-nament when the organisers at Toby's Grandmother's club were caught short.

But that had all been years ago. Toby had gravitated to the management track, which meant he could be involved in just about any sport.

Garrett glanced at the television screen. "Cricket?"

"No."

He mentally whizzed through all of Toby's preferred summer sports. "Swimming?"

"Nu-uh."

"Volleyball?"

"Nope."

Grr. Had Toby always been this annoying? "What, then?"

"Tennis. I'm the tournament director for the Queensland Championship Cup."

That took him aback. "Director? Are you serious? Isn't that an ATP tournament?" Toby couldn't hit a tennis ball to save his own life.

"I know, I know. Good thing being skilled at the sport isn't a prerequisite to officiate...or to manage a tournament."

A fact Garrett well knew, but that didn't make his old friend's rise any less incredible...or any less of a gut punch when viewed against the demise of his own career.

"Congrats," he gritted out.

Meaning it.

Just.

"Thanks. Anyway. To cut to the chase, I'm short a few line umpires. A whole group were supposed to fly over after the last platinum tournament of the year in Perth, but they all went to the same new year's party and caught a nasty stomach bug. Don't ask me what. I do *not* want to know."

Typical Toby—always squeamish.

"And you want me to fill in?" Was the man insane?

Did Toby know nothing about his current condition? About his injuries?

"You still help your dad out in the footy off-season, don't you? He still running that regional comp?" Toby asked.

"Yeah. But behind the scenes." How many years had it been since he'd called the lines on a tennis court? At least four. When he got the nod to referee for the AFL—the biggest sporting stage in the nation—he'd put blinders on to every other sport. "Toby, I haven't line umpired for years. I couldn't even tell you how rusty I am."

"Don't be ridiculous. I don't care if it's a tennis ball, a soccer ball, or a bloody bowling ball, you could read the path of a ball in your sleep."

But that was then.

Before.

All it had taken was one idiot teenager, driving high, for everything good—everything Garrett had worked toward—to be ripped away.

Not his life, though. That he still had, such that it was.

The surgeons had done what they could to put his Humpty Dumpty body back together, and Kevin had soon got him moving again, but his life wasn't repaired.

No way could he go back to how things used to be. But Garrett couldn't figure out how to go forward. Where to go. Or even who to be. Not without footy.

Without footy.

Jesus, could he be any more of a sad sack?

Just the thought of starting all over again made his gut cramp.

He couldn't lie on his sofa and watch the clouds drift by forever. But what was the alternative?

"Is your registration with Tennis Australia still active?"

"I think so. No reason for it to be revoked. But my rank must be in the basement by now. I don't know if I even qualify to umpire at an ATP tournament."

"Have you had an eye exam in the past year?" Toby ignored his protest. "Still twenty-twenty?"

"Yeah, of course, but..." Garrett's voice drifted away.

What could he say?

My eyes are fine, it's just the rest of me that's a problem.

Hell, no.

"I can't be still for too long." Not without every muscle seizing up.

Wait, am I actually thinking about this?

Was he really so desperate for life to get back to normal that he'd agree to Toby's ridiculous request? The idea that he'd fly half-way up the country to stand on a hard tennis court and stare at a white line for hours was ludicrous. Wasn't it?

"Yes," he answered his own question. Yes, it was.

"Great. Thanks, Garrett. You're a lifesaver."

"Wait! No. That's not what I—"

But Toby didn't wait.

"Get your arse up here. Today if you can. Sunday at the latest. Everyone's starting Monday on a seven-day contract. You can stay with me," he said, his choppy words betraying his anxiety.

"Wait!" Garrett sat forward on the edge of the seat.

"Nah, it'll be fine. Hamish won't mind. He's secure in our marriage. Just let me know your flight details as soon as you're sorted. I'll send one of the volunteer drivers to get you out to the stadium at Tennyson."

"Toby, wait!" Garrett shouted into the phone.

But Toby had hung up.

"Shit."

The steel rods that reinforced half of his spine protested as Garrett slumped down on the sofa.

On his television, the crowd went wild, hooting as the Aussie batsman ripped a ball off the crease and up, up, up into the air. It sailed high over the grass oval, all the way to the boundary where one of the visiting Brits cupped his hands and the red leather ball landed, cradled safe in his grasp.

"Shit," Garrett repeated.

What the ever-loving hell had he gotten himself into?

CHAPTER TWO

Spencer

"Eyes on the ball. That's it, Amy." Spencer called across the net.

He tracked the wild lob, shuffle-skipped a couple steps into the deuce court, then sent the fluffy yellow ball back in a gentle arc to her backhand.

She double-fisted her racquet, swung, and missed the ball entirely.

"Good try."

Spencer didn't often take novices. His steep hourly fee was usually enough to discourage them. But Amy, sporting her flashy Lacoste outfit and pro-level Wilson racquet, wasn't limited by finances. Plus, she owned the apartment at Tennyson Bend where Spencer lived, rent-free, for the duration of his tenure as player-in-residence at the state tennis centre. The least he could do to return the favour was coach her for an hour or so whenever his tournament schedule allowed.

He pulled another ball from his pocket and drop-hit it. It sailed over the net and bounced on the exact same spot as the previous ball.

"Try again."

Again.

That was tennis.

Practice. Practice. Practice.

Again, and again, and again.

Sometimes Spencer thought he'd fucking smash someone the next time he heard that word—put a ball straight through their head. Tennis balls weren't the best projectile, but they could do serious damage if hit hard enough, with skill and precision.

Just ask his junior coach at the academy who was always shooting balls at his head.

"Teaching you to move, Bloom," he'd always say.

Yeah, right.

Spencer's years there had almost killed his love of the game. Almost...but not quite.

Day after day, hour after hour, ball after ball after ball.

Again. Again. Again.

Till the game became second nature. Part of his flesh and bones.

From that first year at the academy, aged scrawny-ten, he'd return home for a week every Christmas from Queensland's Gold Coast in the east, to Perth in the west. And every year he'd receive from Santa new-season tennis gear and an annual Champions of Tennis calendar. He'd fill the squares below the action shots of his heroes with all the happenings at home—everything he'd miss as he pressed ever forward toward the goal of becoming a pro tennis player.

He imagined one day holding the Australian Open trophy high in the air and called it his dream.

The Plan—his mum called it—capital T, capital P.

'Win,' she'd say as she and his dad waved him off at Perth Airport to fly the three-thousand-plus kilometres back across the country. 'Go make us proud.'

Spencer's heartbeat hitched at the memory, and the toe of his shoe caught on the surface of the night-lit hardcourt. He recovered fast. Instinct drove his left foot down and he modified his stroke to flick the ball with a hint of topspin. It dropped exactly where he'd originally intended, trip or not.

The shot wasn't graceful. Not how he'd been trained to play. But it'd do while he coached Amy. It wasn't as if he was out on centre court, his every move televised live, dissected by commentators, judged by the public.

Not yet.

Amy swung and hit the ball clean. It flew low over the net and into Spencer's ad court.

He didn't run after it. Just let it bounce and sail into the chain-link fence at the back of the court.

"Winner!" She raised her arms.

"Excellent, Amy. You're really starting to get it. How about we end on a high?" Any other day, he'd stick around for a casual hit with his student. Have a little fun. But the up-coming twenty-four hours were too important to waste messing around.

"Sure, Coach. Same time next week?" Amy asked, but before he could say no, she said, "Oh! Wait! You can't. Silly me. I almost forgot." She winked.

As though Amy could have forgotten…

As though anyone living in the Tennyson Bend apartment building across the road from the state tennis centre could forget that the Queensland Championship Cup was about to begin, and that, after years in the ITP and Challenger wilderness, he'd get his chance at a major ATP tournament.

Finally.

"Tease," he accused.

She grinned, did a girlish twirl in her pleated tennis skirt, and started rounding up the dozens of balls that speckled her end of the court like neon yellow confetti.

He turned to do the same at his end. The task was laborious, but it always felt good to Spencer—a moment to come back into himself, to breathe easy and clear his thoughts.

They parted ways at the tennis centre café, where Amy met up with some of her let's-do-lunch friends, and he returned the basket of balls to his coach's cupboard in the training rooms beneath the main stadium. He closed the door, turned the key, and tapped once on the *Coach Bloom* sign. The simple laminated sheet of paper was hardly a grand slam trophy, but it gave him a warm fuzzy sense of accomplishment every time he saw it.

From there, it was a quick walk out of the training rooms to the subterranean tunnel that shot under the road between the tennis centre and Tennyson Bend, then up the elevator to his sixth-floor apartment.

Once home, Spencer flipped the shower faucet to hot, then stripped off his staff polo shirt, toed off his right shoe, and had his shorts and undies halfway down when Queen's "We Are the Champions" jangled from his mobile phone.

"Shit."

He tried to get everything off over his left shoe, but they tightened like a lasso around his ankle. He gave up and shuffle-hopped across his bedroom to grab his mobile phone from the pocket of his tennis bag.

"Hey, Mum."

"You're breathless. Why are you breathless? You're not sick, are you? What's your temperature? Have you seen a doctor? What does Kaz think? Make sure you—"

"I'm fine, Mum." Spencer broke through her anxious tirade. If he didn't, she could coddle for hours. Not real coddling, mind. Spencer couldn't remember the last time he'd had a real, earnest, caring hug from either of his parents. Just an abundance of concern for his ability to perform. "I've just run in after a session with a student. No big deal."

"You shouldn't let them take so much from you, Spencer. Reserve your energy for what's truly important. Don't waste your talent."

There it was—*talent*—his very own personal swear word. If he could remove it from the dictionary, he would.

That and *win*.

You're so talented, Spencer. You're a winner!

They expected nothing less.

Time for a diversion, Bloom.

Spencer finally managed to toe off the last shoe with his shorts. In nothing but socks, he padded down the hall to his open-plan kitchen-dining-lounge room.

"What did you and Dad get up to for New Years? And Casey and Bryce? Any plans for this week?" He ought to know the answers to those questions, Spencer thought. He ought to know what everyone in his family was doing over the holidays. Wasn't that what families were usually like? All up in each other's business? Invested in the minutiae of their daily lives?

"Your father and I went to the Stewart's house last night to watch the New Year's Eve fireworks. A lovely evening."

On the other side of the kitchen island, Spencer uncapped a black marker and hovered in front of the new calendar he'd pinned to the wall.

He was about to write *Stewart's NYE Party* on December thirty-first, when she said, "Shame you had to miss it." Her words came blithely, as though he'd ever been given the choice. He saw red.

Miss it? "I wasn't invited."

"Don't be like that, Spencer."

"Like what?"

"Bitter. You've got far better things to do than hang out at some party drinking Champagne. That's not part of the plan."

Oh, yeah. How could he forget *The Plan*?

"Did Casey and Bryce go?"

"Well, yes. Of course, they did. They couldn't very well be left out when the party's right next door."

"Of course not." He recapped the marker and stepped back, but he didn't take his eyes off the as-yet-unmarked January first square.

For so many years he'd habitually filled in the spaces with everything he hadn't done. Everything he *couldn't* attend because he was so far away from home. Every now and then, when life got hard, and when success seemed about as distant as the moon, he'd flick through his old Champions of Tennis calendars and remind himself of all that he'd given up to pursue the dream.

Number one.

Spencer knew that in his mum's one-track mind those words were as true a claim as *you don't need to be home to be happy.*

It was true that *home* and *happy* weren't mutually exclusive, but he'd lived that life—roamed Australia and the world with his coach on speed-dial, scraping by on the ITF and Challenger circuits, trading hits with other hopefuls, just like him.

Step by step, slowly but surely, he'd inched up the ATP world rankings.

Big triple figures.

Mid triple figures.

Knocking on the door of double figures.

"I'm sure you'll do brilliantly, darling. Hometown hero and all that."

"Hometown hero?"

"Well, you do live in Brisbane now."

He supposed that was true, but it was jarring to think of any place other than Perth as home.

"And centre court! Imagine that. Our Spencer."

Centre court…playing the tournament's number one seed…in front of thousands.

"We'll be watching, darling."

Shit.

"And Kaz's family is coming around, since we've got the big screen."

"Coach's family will be there too? Does he know?"

"Of course. We all wanted to fly over and support you in your player's box, but it's a bit far to come for one match, darling. We'll be with you in spirit."

Meaning none of them thought he'd make it past the first round.

Great. Just great.

"I appreciate everyone's encouragement Mum, but—" How could he tell her it felt like a ten-tonne yoke around his neck?

"Casey even made a digital banner for you. She'll add it to your socials."

"I don't do social media." He couldn't think of much worse than having strangers privy to his business, personal or otherwise.

"Your sister made it for you. Isn't that sweet?"

Sweet isn't the word I'd use. "In my name?"

"Of course, in your name, silly. It's your fan page."

Fan page? What the hell?

He glared at the empty square on the calendar. "I didn't agree to that."

"No?"

He rubbed at his sternum with his knuckles, and said firmly, "No."

The fucking square could stay blank.

"Spencer!" he heard the tinny voice of his mum yelling his name, probably not for the first time. "Don't ignore your mother!"

How long had he stared at that empty square?

"Sorry, Mum. Gotta go to training," Spencer said, then hung up. His conscience twinged, but it was only a little white lie. Surely the universe would forgive him for that.

Spencer glanced back up at the calendar's January Champion of Tennis image.

The sweat-sheened face of the number twelve in the world stared back at him. Did Shawn O'Connell have to deal with the same shit from his family? He wondered.

Some people said they looked alike, but Spencer couldn't see it.

Sure, he had the same ridiculous height, the sharp cheekbones, the too-long hair, and the scraggly scruff that didn't know if it wanted to be a beard or not; but Spencer's tan wasn't made of freckles, his messy mop was dirtier than Shawn's strawberry blonde, and there were two decimal places between their respective ATP rankings. Other than those minor differences, Spencer supposed he could see why people got them confused.

He shifted his gaze to the next empty square—January 2—and wrote:

11 a.m. – Centre Court

Spencer Bloom (127) v Javier Centaurini (1)

His chance had finally come.

Spencer recapped the marker and stepped back.

He pulled on a dry pair of running shoes, shorts, and a loose tank top, yanked open his front door, and headed out into the muggy summer night.

Time to make his own dreams come true.

CHAPTER THREE

Garrett

The wall of mirrors gave the impression of more space in the stadium gym, reflecting rows and rows of static cardio and weight machines, free-weights, yoga mats, and the familiar series of anatomical posters depicting the components of a healthy, fully-functioning human body.

Garrett's image was reflected, too. Not that he cared if anyone noticed him. He didn't give a shit if anyone judged his snail-like speed as he walked the treadmill at a steady three-point-five kilometres per hour.

Late on a Sunday night, few people were around to witness the painful regimen Kevin had promised would get his body closer to recovery.

Before his accident, four kilometres per hour wouldn't've even registered as a warm-up.

After, he was just glad he could walk at all.

Garrett slicked the beads of perspiration from his forehead, upped the speed of the treadmill by a tenth of a kilometre, and paced on. He barely spared a glance for two woman doing free-weights in the corner, or for the middle-aged guy on the rowing machine beside him who grunted, red-faced, with each rhythmic pull.

Garrett tuned them out—just like he did his best to tune out every nerve twinge, muscle strain, and bone-deep throb that tried to stop him in his tracks.

When a hot streak of pain flared down his right leg, he didn't need to check out the anatomy posters to know it was his lumbar spine protesting. He just upped the incline a few degrees to lessen the shock of each footfall.

Fucking orthopaedic surgeons.

At barely half way through the prescribed distance, the main door to the gym opened and a man walked in.

He dripped with sweat, too.

Except that was where the similarities between them ended.

For starters, the man looked a good ten years younger. Though, given how Garrett's body felt about a hundred years old, he figured he probably wasn't the greatest judge of age.

Smooth skin tanned gold by the sun, he looked like Achilles, fresh from battle in Troy.

Also, he was tall—tall enough to instinctively duck his head through the doorway, which made his medusa-messy, long blonde hair swing forward and cover half his face.

Rivetted to the man's reflection, Garrett watched him absently finger-comb his sweat-darkened locks back, revealing a strong, corded neck and defined collarbone. He pulled a band from around his wrist and twisted his hair up into a man bun at the crown of his head. The simple move flexed all the muscles of his upper body and, in the large gaps left bare by his loose tank top, Garrett caught a flash of pit hair, inky with perspiration.

Was he a local member of the gym? Someone on staff at the tennis centre? Or a pro tennis player in town for Toby's tournament?

He looked more than fit enough to be the latter, but Garrett didn't recognise him. Not that he knew all the players by face. Or by name. It'd been ages since he'd paid enough attention to the sport to have that kind of detail at his fingertips.

As the man walked to the water cooler by the entrance to the locker room, Garrett tracked the man's movements in the mirror.

The ladies lifting weights in the corner called out to him.

Achilles waved back, but didn't engage further.

Then he bent over to drink.

Garrett's step stuttered—his left foot caught on the rubber runner. In a split second, the motion of the treadmill pulled his hips backward, which yanked the kill-switch clipped to the bottom of his t-shirt and brought the rubber runner to an abrupt halt. Momentum carried his torso forward and he face-planted straight into the control panel. "Gah!" he doubled over, one hand covering his face, the other clenched tight to the treadmill handlebar, and he shook with the effort of holding his dead-weight up.

The rower guy stopped mid pull. "You alright, mate?"

"Yeah." Garrett dismissed his concern. What else could he say without embarrassing himself further? *I just about killed myself lusting after a man way out of my league?*

Hell, no.

A drip fell to the treadmill, darkening the matte rubber surface. Was it sweat, or...?

He pulled his knuckles away from his nose. His luck it'd be spouting blood like a fucking firehose.

Everything hurt, but that wasn't new. He groaned as he exerted every bit of willpower in his body to stay on his feet.

And then there were hands on him. Fingers splayed wide around his ribs.

"Don't." He sucked in a harsh breath as the move wrenched bone-deep hurts. After months of rehab, the ability to stand alone was hard won. Garrett wasn't in a hurry to relinquish that ever again. He didn't like anyone trying to hold him up.

His thighs shuddered with the effort as he released his death-grip on the treadmill bar and straightened. Then he turned to see who was attached to the helpful-not-helpful hands.

Jesus.

It was him.

Half warrior, half God.

Up close.

Well inside his personal space.

"You alright, mate?" Achilles asked.

"Yeah." *No. Not okay. Come back. Touch me again.*

The hands were back.

Hallelujah.

They gently smoothed across his forehead, around his temples, and over his cheekbones, the pads of his fingers palpated gently up the bridge of his nose. "Doesn't feel like it's broken,"

Achilles murmured, and Garrett got a whiff of fresh minty toothpaste.

Nice.

Except it made him want to know what the man smelled like for real. Which was ridiculous.

Since when did he go around smelling people?

Even if they were sexy as fuck.

Garrett experimentally twitched his nose. It hurt, but...yeah, not broken.

The fingers traced back down the side of his nose and under his left eye. Gentle.

It stilled him.

Garrett didn't move a muscle, but every cell inside his body seemed to shift when the tall man's gaze met his.

Green eyes.

Soft green—like lichen—surrounded by cork-brown lashes.

Garrett couldn't look away. And when the man took a step sideways, Garrett's body swayed too, making him stumble. Again.

Shit.

"Woah." The hand whipped down to cup Garrett's elbow.

Jesus. When did I become such a wilting violet?

"Is he alright?" The rowing man didn't get off of his machine, thank goodness.

"I'm fine." Garrett wished with all his might that it was true.

A frown line appeared between those eyes. "Maybe so, but there's no point pushing it. Let's go find you some ice."

Don't push it? What else am I supposed to do? If I don't push it, I'll get nowhere.

Garrett let a little of his weight fall into that strong, callused hand.

It wasn't weakness, per se...

He wasn't feeble.

He didn't need the man's help.

But he was weak for the man's touch.

"Lead on," Garrett said, willing to take the risk.

CHAPTER FOUR

Spencer

"Are you supposed to be in here?" The guy's step stuttered and he pointed at the *staff only* sign on the door they'd come through to the treatment rooms.

"Don't worry about it," Spencer said. His words seemed to be enough to appease the guy's worry. Or perhaps he was just quiet because of the donk to his head. Did he have a concussion?

God, I hope not.

"I'm a tennis coach," Spencer added. "Nothing too impressive." Which was true. Or, at least, partly true. The words *I'm a pro*, were true, too, but for some reason those words wouldn't come out of Spencer's mouth. It felt easier to be an innocuous coach for a bit longer. Not a player. Not someone burdened with the yoke of expectation.

Even though he was.

For the first time, in a few short hours, he'd play on live television for all the tennis-watching world to see—to judge, and, probably, to witness his execution at the hands of Javier

Centaurini—*numero uno; sekai ranku ichi; nummer eins; world number one*—The Centaur.

Spencer squared his shoulders.

The way the gorgeous guy from the gym was looking at him—with a vague sort of Zen horn-dog look—it didn't matter that Spencer was the lowest ranked male player in the tournament. A man didn't need to be number one to rate as a human.

Clearly, he didn't recognise Spencer's face, which felt...nice.

"That explains the ladies," the guy said.

Spencer frowned. "What ladies?"

The guy pointed his thumb back down the corridor. "The two women in the gym. They seemed to...know you."

"Know me?" Spencer asked.

The guy shrugged. "Like you."

Like me? Was the guy fishing?

"I've given Amy a few lessons. I like her fine, but I wouldn't say that I know her. Or that she really knows me."

The guy.

Jesus, Spencer hadn't even been decent enough to ask him his name.

Except, if he had asked him his name, Spencer would have to offer his own.

Bye, bye anonymity.

Bye, bye opportunity to simply be himself.

He didn't have much of a public image. Not yet. But fame came with success. That was how the tennis world worked. Spencer was more than ready for success. He wanted to be recognised for his skill, not fame or notoriety. He didn't give a shit about them.

Spencer tightened his grip on the guy's elbow and propelled him further down the hall, through the deserted trainer's gym, and into one of the treatment rooms where the medicos and physios kept their gear. He made a beeline for the bar fridge in the corner and grabbed a bright blue gel pack from the freezer section.

The guy touched his left hand to his face.

"Is it hurting? Here. Ice will help." Spencer scrunched and smoothed the cold gel pack into the right shape, then batted the guy's hand away and placed the pack gently over the bridge of his nose.

The guy winced at the chill. When he went cross-eyed looking down it, Spencer had to purse his lips to hold in a laugh.

So cute.

"You've done that a few times," came the guy's muffled voice.

"Iced a nose? Occupational hazard. Although, I think this is the first time I've had to give first aid for a treadmill face plant."

The guy groaned. "Can we please forget that ever happened?"

"Sure." Spencer couldn't keep the twist from his lips. If the guy thought he could forget it, he was sorely mistaken.

The guy pulled it away from his nose for a quick glance at it, then put it back in place. "You've got the form right. Feels perfectly cradled."

"I'm familiar with the anatomy." Spencer touched the tip of his own nose, but the guy wasn't looking at Spencer's face.

He was looking down.

Spencer dipped his knees to check out the guy's eyes.

Underneath heavy lids, his pupils looked blown, surrounded by a tiny corona.

Spencer tried to remember if that meant he might be concussed or...

Could he be aroused?

He replayed their conversation in his head. Suddenly, the
word 'anatomy' seemed like it should have an adults-only rating.

Had he been flirting with me all along?

Spencer inhaled deep through his nose as he straightened up.

Which of course made it sound like he was sniffing the guy.
Deep.

And then, somehow, they were a few inches closer.

Which was perfectly fine with Spencer, except...what if the
guy didn't know what he was doing? What if he *was* concussed?

Do not lust after the guy with the suspected head injury.

Only, it was way too late to act on that wise gem of a thought,
because within a blink their chests were barely a hair-width
apart.

Wait, did I move? Or did he?

"What else do you know well enough to form an anatomical
fit?" the guy asked.

Memories of sports physiology text books raced through his
mind, but something told him that wasn't what the guy was
getting at.

Spencer tried to collect himself but failed.

"Um." *Cool, Bloom. So cool.*

Luckily, the guy didn't seem to care about his non-answer.

"Ever had a fantasy about getting it on in the locker room?"

Oh, good. An easy question. "Yeah," was the simple answer,
because that particular fantasy had found a home in his spank
bank at the onset of puberty.

Technically, they weren't in the locker room.

But, maybe, if...

He heard the gel pack drop to the floor and the guy closed the infinitesimal gap between them.

"Oh."

Hands touched him. Fingertips trailed up his biceps, deltoids, up the taper of his trapezius, and stopped where his carotid thrummed. A thumb touched gently to Spencer's Adams apple and rode the wave of a hard swallow.

How could he be near-drooling one second, and parch-mouthed the next?

"I like your bun," the guy said.

"Huh?"

Fingertips tickled Spencer's skin at the base of his neck and combed up to the crown of his head. "Your hipster man bun."

"It's not a man bun."

"Yes, it is."

"No, it isn't. It's a top knot, or a club."

The thumb shoved at his jaw to get Spencer to turn his head for a better view. "As in a bash-me-over-my-head-and-take-me-back-to-your-cave-type club?"

Umm. "No?"

The fingertips kept moving. "Are you sure? Because that sounds kind of wild right about now."

"I'm not really the caveman type."

"More sophisticated than that, eh? Not your usual approach to seduction?"

"No...well..." Spencer's words came to a stuttering halt. How could he claim an approach to seduction when he'd never really seduced anyone?

Over the years, he'd met a few like-minded guys on the circuit. It was always easy—make eye contact, sneak between hotel rooms, trade a hand, or a mouth, or a quick fuck, move on—nothing frantic, no deep feelings, no holy-mother-of-God-is-this-man-for-real type sex. No seduction necessary.

So, no...not sophisticated.

What was his other option?

Caveman?

That set the bar pretty low.

Unevolved?

Stunted in the art of being human?

A *bash-you-over-the-head-and-take-you-back-to-my-cave-type* guy?

Technically, Spencer supposed he *had* dragged the stranger (gently, by the elbow) back to his cave (well, the treatment rooms weren't technically his, but so late on a Sunday night the chance of them being interrupted was pretty damn low).

Not that that had been his intent. It was the guy's injuries he was concerned about. Or, had been...then.

God. He couldn't think straight with the guy so up close and kissable.

Kissing. Mmm.

What if he did act the caveman?

No civility.

No nicety.

Only animal instinct.

Which was telling him right that second to...

Spencer swooped in for a kiss—a teeth-clacking, tongue-sucking, earth-shattering kiss.

And it was wild.

CHAPTER FIVE

Garrett

Between the jaunty alarm set at a thousand decibels and the rabid vibration that made his phone jigger-jigger across the bedside table, Garrett could have happily thrown the fucking thing into another dimension. If he could untangle himself from the sweaty sheets to reach it, that was.

The minute he managed to roll over and grabbed the phone to shut off the obnoxious alarm, he regretted that action too. He'd forgotten to close the guest-room blinds, so streaks of white-hot sunlight lashed diagonally across the bed and sliced like shards of glass into his eyes.

He grabbed a pillow to press against his face and cursed into the softness as every single second of the night's events rushed back in.

"Hell." A kiss like that shouldn't have stuck in his mind.

It had been hot as fuck, but also kind of awkward. If his Achilles hadn't looked and felt like a full-grown man, Garrett might have thought him a novice.

He'd shoved Garrett up against a massage table and ground against him like a horny teen on a first date. Enthusiastic, but un-practiced. Which was why, in Garrett's humble opinion, he ought to have been able to forget all about it.

Except, he hadn't.

Hell, he probably would've taken it a whole lot further if they hadn't been interrupted.

His Achilles had raced away so fast that Garrett wondered if he actually *was* famed Achilles, as he left Garrett to explain to the security guard that yes, he was staff, that, yes, he was allowed into restricted areas of the tennis centre, and that no, there was no need to call the tournament director to confirm his employment status.

Half-awake Toby had not been impressed.

Nor, when they finally got back to their town home, was Toby's husband Hamish.

Falling asleep had been near impossible, his dreams kept him rock hard, and his sleep alarm felt like the final nail on the coffin of his sanity. Finally awake, Garrett shoved the bedding off, gritty eyed, still tense with need, and very, very late.

Toby was going to kill him.

Again.

Neither Toby nor Hamish were anywhere in sight, so Garrett threw back a couple Ibuprofen, grabbed his gear, and flew out the door.

The ten-minute Uber ride to the tennis centre gave Garrett far too much time to fall back into memories of the kiss. Frantic fumbling like that couldn't be faked. Hell, nobody *would* fake it. Not on purpose. It was endearing, and he wanted more.

If Garrett ran into his Achilles again, he'd suggest they hook up while he was in town.

Garrett wasn't up for anything emotionally or physically athletic, but a week-long screw sounded far more therapeutic than Kevin's regimen. A week was far too short a time to worry about emotional entanglements. He was about as likely to fall for the guy as he was to get offered the chair umpire position at the Australian Open men's final—zip, zero, none. To fall for someone, he had to trust them, and how could he trust anyone who ran away at the first hint of discovery?

His Achilles was clearly a flight risk.

Normally, that would put him well off of Garrett's radar.

Normally.

But there was nothing much normal about Garrett's life anymore.

With his temporary staff card, Garrett scanned through the security gate, then headed down to the subterranean rabbit warren beneath the stadium. He held on tight to the rail as he stiffly made his way down the stairs. The pain killers were starting to kick in, but he'd need a dedicated masseuse if he didn't want to creak twenty-four seven.

Fresh off the plane the night before, Toby had given him a quick tour of the tennis centre, so he had a basic idea of where to go. But the stadium had a different feel when thousands of visitors swarmed the grounds and the stadium above—charged up for the first round of the tournament.

Garrett rushed down the main fish-spine corridor to the door grandiosely marked *Officials' Antechamber* at the polar end. Then he stopped, suddenly heavy with indecision.

Given how much of a soap opera the tennis world was—how up in each other's business officials were—Garrett was in little doubt that the people on the other side of that door would form judgements before he could say much more than "boo!" Which meant he had a short window of opportunity to dictate terms.

Thanks to Toby, he'd made it back. Not all the way back...but enough of the way to feel something closer to normal than he'd felt for months. He owed the man for that renewed sense of purpose. No way would Garrett leave him in the lurch.

'Normal', though, brought expectations that he wasn't quite sure he could live up to.

He could put on his game face, walk through that door, and not be known as a broken man.

But, could he live up to it?

When it came to pro-tennis umpiring, Garrett was two-parts old hack, one-part green horn. It wasn't rocket science to focus on the line and voice the call, but it'd been a while. He was rusty.

Garrett could only hope they'd set him up somewhere low profile. Ease him in, so that he could arrive looking shiny and new—like a toy on Christmas morning with all its parts in working order—rather than the rusty tinman he'd become.

Buck up, arsehole. It's time.

Garrett rolled his neck, making his spine grind like gravel rash and a wave of nausea ripple through him. He clenched his fists at his sides, then splayed his fingers wide, imagining shards of electricity sparking to earth, grounding himself in the moment.

Then he squared his shoulders, turned the knob, and pushed the door open.

The room was awash with taupe trousers and sky-blue polo shirts. Garrett felt like the new kid at school when everyone was all matchy-matchy in their uniforms.

He'd forgotten how big of an operation a tournament the size of the Queensland Championship Cup was. Nothing massive like a grand slam, of course, but at the open ATP level every match required a chair umpire, a net umpire, eighteen rotating line umpires, and a bevy of ball kids. Add roving court supervisors and tournament referees and the numbers added up, fast.

He didn't count heads, but Garrett figured there must have been a couple hundred people crammed into the room, listening to Toby give his characteristic ra-ra speech of dedication and responsibility and "let's have fun, team!"

As soon as Toby wound up, he made a bee-line for Garrett.

"You alright?" he asked. "Everything okay?"

"Yeah. Sorry. Forgot you Queenslanders don't do daylight saving." It wasn't a lie—not entirely. He had forgotten to adjust his phone's clock settings back an hour, but that wasn't what had kept him awake half the night. "I'll have the old body clock sorted by tomorrow."

"Sure. Good. No problem." Toby mimicked Garrett's hands in his pockets and rocked back onto his heels.

Figuring it was a subliminal attempt to show him empathy, Garrett decided to have a little fun.

He rubbed his tummy with one hand.

Toby did it too.

Then he lifted his other hand and scratched his nose.

Toby half lifted his other hand, then stopped himself. "Funny," he grimaced.

Garrett snorted. "That'll teach you not to use your sensitivity training management techniques on me."

Toby's nostrils flared. "Why'd I ever call you for help?"

"God knows." Garrett hid his hands in his pockets and pointed his chin to the platform where Toby had stood to give his speech. "What did I miss? Anything important?" As much as he was loving giving Toby shit, the man had a job to do, and so did he.

"Just a few crucial things," Toby said, dry as could be.

"So...you'll send me the memo?"

"Mm-hmm, I'll get my secretary right on that."

"Excellent. So...how does this thing work?"

Toby sighed. "Ruth Whitlock, the head referee, assigned everyone randomly into five line-umpire crews—alpha, beta, gamma, delta, and epsilon. You're in the gamma crew."

"Damn. Doesn't the universe realise I'm supposed to be alpha?"

Toby ignored him. "Come Thursday, we'll reset into three crews based on your official tournament rank, then taper off to the two crews we need for the finals on Saturday and Sunday, day and night. Make sense?"

"So far." Garrett nodded. "Where's the gamma squad allocated today?"

"Crew, not squad." Toby flashed a grin. "And gamma is allocated to centre court. Come on...I'll introduce you." He gestured Garrett to follow and took off across the crowded room.

Centre court?

Are you shitting me?

"Hey! Hold up!"

No way could Toby be serious.

CHAPTER SIX

Garrett

Turned out Toby *was* entirely serious.

While play got underway in the arena above their heads, Garrett did his best to relax in the officials' antechamber with the second half of Gamma crew.

Cate, one of his line-mates, twisted to face him on the sofa seat beside him.

"Nervous?" she asked.

"Only to a point." Garrett prevaricated, wishing she'd drop it.

"And what point might that be?"

He waggled his hand. "Maybe to the point of nausea."

Cate patted his knee. "That's perfectly normal. You'll be okay." His line-mate was a coddler, which would normally piss Garrett off no end. He already had one decent parent; he didn't need another. But any distraction was good. In seven games, he'd be out there on centre court, calling the shots on Javier Centaurini, the number one player in the world.

Garrett had confidence in his ability.

He did.

He trusted his eyes. He trusted his focus. And he trusted his quick judgment. But what bit of universal fuckery had him calling the line for Javier Centaurini?

The gods must have been howling.

It was unethical for any umpire to show favouritism, but Garrett sympathised with the poor unseeded player pitted against Javier—some local guy by the name of Spencer Bloom. Probably just out of juniors. Garrett hadn't heard of him, but that wasn't all that surprising.

"How many games till we swap out with the other half of the crew?" he asked, unable to bring himself to look at the muted flat screen mounted on the wall above their heads.

She contorted herself to have a look.

"Four...no, three games. Oh, dear. Poor Spencer. Five-love. He's getting trounced." She stood away from their sofa to get a better view.

He stood to join her, but what he saw wasn't the gangly seventeen-year-old upstart he expected. "Holy shit!"

"I know, right. If I was twenty years younger." Cate fanned herself with a hand. "We're supposed to be impartial, but I so wanted Spencer to do well. Poor guy, can't catch a break...or barely a point, it would seem. Look at Javier. He's not even sweating."

No, but Garrett was.

What were the chances that the man on the screen wasn't the same Achilles look-a-like he'd practically inhaled twelve hours before?

Nil, none, love.

His swirling gut turned to lead. "I need to walk." He didn't wait for Cate to reply, just took off to pace the length of the room. If the score was anything to go by, his half of the gamma crew were due to go on court in a matter of minutes, and there was nowhere to hide on centre court.

Spencer. He tried the man's name out in his mind, then on his tongue, "Spencer."

As he paced by, he took a quick glance at the screen.

"Spencer Bloom," he read aloud, but it wasn't the guy's name his attention snagged on. The camera operator had zeroed in Spencer's face—on the beads of sweat, and the ragged locks of hair, and the furrow between his brows.

"Grown up nice, hasn't he?"

Garrett jolted in surprise at Cate's presence by his shoulder. "Way to sneak up on a man," he grated out.

She chuckled. "As though that's what's got you all hot and bothered."

He gave her a *what could you possibly mean?* look.

In return, she gave him a mumsy *don't even think about touching that tempting bit of man-flesh* look, which should have been entirely unnecessary. Garrett was a professional. Except he'd already touched. He'd touched a whole goddamn lot. And he wanted to touch more.

He looked away from her far-too-knowing expression, and back to the television.

In the top left corner of the screen, the score may as well have read "dire strife" instead of *5-0* in Centaurini's favour, but Garrett wasn't watching that. His attention followed the lean lines of Spencer's body, riddled with tension as he positioned his left toe at the baseline to serve. His sun-licked hair had half fallen out of his man bun to graze shoulders hiked so high he could have worn them as earphones.

"Relax," Garrett said to the screen, willing the man to take a moment to collect himself.

At *15-40*, if he lost his next serve, he'd lose the set.

Fault.

"Again," Garrett whispered.

He couldn't see Spencer's eyes, but Garrett somehow knew they'd be oh so sharp with grit and intent. Spencer Bloom may not have been a true contender for the tournament crown, but he wasn't giving up without a fight.

Good boy.

Spencer squeezed his racquet handle in his fist, bounced the tennis ball twice, swayed back onto his heels, then, in a frenetic whirl, he tossed the ball and whipped his racquet up and around and through it, his momentum driving him forward, deep into the court.

In.

Yes!

Long legs took Spencer to the net quick enough to snap the return backhand into the deuce corner, but Centaurini was on it—his forehand taking it low, and it spun back at an insane angle, whippet fast.

Spencer stretched sideways. His body straining to reach the low volley.

He's there!

But, *nick!* the ball clipped the net, sheered it off its sharp trajectory, and it arced up and over Spencer's racquet head.

Time seemed to suspend. Garrett's eyes stayed glued to the tiny yellow ball of fluff as it arced—painfully slow, and oh so fast—up and over and deep into the court. Too deep for Spencer to have any hope of getting it.

Game, and first set to The Centaur.

The score board in the top left corner of the screen flipped.

Six-love.

"Shit."

The ball kids started their rhythmic dance, sending the balls to the other end for the change of service, and Garrett closed his eyes and turned away.

What to do?

If he went out there, could he do his job without compromising the integrity of the match?

Official rules and standards of professional integrity demanded he should have spoken up the minute he recognised Spencer as his Achilles. It was a clear conflict of interest. Just because he hadn't known the man was a fucking tennis player when they'd kissed, that didn't absolve him of his ethical responsibility.

But, had they really made a personal connection?

Physical didn't always mean intimate.

They'd not even traded names, for fuck's sake.

And, he wanted to help, goddamn it—to stand by Spencer's side.

That errant thought brought him up short. "Jesus, Fellows." His instinctive support for the man was a clear red flag.

"What was that, Garrett?" Cate asked.

He shook his head and started his pacing again.

If he couldn't find a way to be impartial, he was screwed.

Oh, who was he kidding? He was already screwed. "Never mind red flag—may as well fly the white flag," he muttered to himself.

Which was the exact reason why he shouldn't go up there on court, he told himself.

Impartiality. That was the name of the game for referees...and the great contradiction. Love the sport, but don't be a fan, and, certainly, don't play favourites.

Was it really bias to wish a player well? To hope he didn't fall flat on his proverbial face?

Of all people, he was an expert in that. As Spencer knew all too well.

"Gear up, gamma crew!" Ruth, the head referee, called from over by the base of the stairwell that would take them up to court level.

"You sure you're okay, Garrett?" Cate touched his forearm. "You look like you've seen a ghost."

No. No, I'm not.

The truth was stuck somewhere between his conscience and his tongue.

What are you doing, Fellows? Don't screw with your career.

But tennis isn't my career.

Not the one you love.

Not the one you've lost.

So...are you alright?

No, I'm not, but... "Yeah," Garrett finally answered.

"Great. Let's get this show on the road, then, shall we?"

He held up his palm to indicate she should lead the way to gather with their half of gamma crew. They were all quiet, but Garrett felt the crew's energy. He wanted to join in—to share the thrill of the match—but he couldn't help dragging his feet the closer he got to the door.

The point of no return.

The time to say something...anything...was fast disappearing.

He could beg off.

Say he was too sore.

Say he wasn't sure he could do the job well enough to make himself, or them, proud.

But, while all those excuses were far too true, none of them were the actual truth of the matter.

The whole truth was Garrett wanted Spencer to have cause to celebrate—cause to seek Garrett out in the dead of night and finish what they'd started.

Garrett had no sway over the first wish coming true, but, if he went up there, his second wish would surely be dashed to smithereens.

And then it was time.

Someone must have radioed through the progressive score, because Ruth tapped her pen on her clipboard to draw the crew's attention.

"Ready?" she asked.

Before he could react, the door opened, the thunder of the crowd's clapping and whistling and stomping roared in, and Garrett was instantly caught in a lie of omission.

"Fuck."

CHAPTER SEVEN

Spencer

Question—how old is too old to throw a tantrum? Spencer asked the universe.

Four? Fourteen? Twenty-four?

Spencer wasn't sure.

And he wasn't talking a passive-aggressive tantrum either.

Spencer jammed his feet forward, making his shoes squeak on the hot surface of the court every single one of the lucky-thirteen steps it took to cross from his seat to the baseline. It wasn't a delaying tactic. The match clock would count down regardless. But he needed to bring the present moment back into solid focus—to make an impact before he lost his grip on the match entirely.

The ball kids at the back of the court buzzed with energy, each of their loaded hands stretched high like a tightly wound trigger, prepared to shoot him a ball at half a nano-second's notice.

It wasn't their fault he was tanking, but he felt so stiff in his own skin, he could barely give each of them a subtle nod of thanks for the balls they bounced his way.

He collected them with a scoop of his racquet head, then took his time to analyse each.

In his saner moments, Spencer would tell anyone that tennis balls weren't inherently lucky or unlucky, but the set they'd been playing with felt like they carried the luck of doom. The dreaded balls wouldn't be swapped out with new ones till after the twelfth game, which meant Spencer only had five miserable games to go before he either stepped up his game and made a contest of it, or suffered catastrophic failure.

A love match.

"Break it down," he mouthed silently to himself. "One grip, one stroke, one play." It wasn't fucking life or death. The universe wasn't going to implode if he lost. But his imminent failure felt dire enough when caught by the magnifying effect of a dozen television cameras, at least half of which were trained directly on him.

He'd not lost to love since the final of his first junior state championship when he and his immature ego had been bundled out by a boy twice his weight and leap-years ahead in tenacity.

Not till the Queensland Championship Cup, against Javier Centaurini, no less.

The Centaur.

The crowd stamped their feet, rattling the entire stadium, willing Spencer on.

They wanted a game, no doubt—a clash worthy of two true competitors.

I'm trying, he wanted to call out in a petulant voice.

In your next life, Bloom, choose doubles. At least then he could share the load of his fuck ups. *Or soccer. Or basketball. Or footy. Or any-fucking-other team sport that'd give him an out from individual blame...*

Or a do-over.

That thought brought him back to the gorgeous face-plant guy whose lung tissue Spencer had practically inhaled the night before.

If he could repeat that effort, Spencer was sure he'd put on a way better performance.

Yep. A do-over there would be good too, because inept shit like that was fucking embarrassing.

It wasn't like Spencer was a virgin or anything. He had no problem finding someone to help scratch that itch. But there was something different about the guy from the gym. He'd made Spencer forget himself, forget where he was, forget his mind, forget his priorities...forget how to choose a fucking ball to serve.

The tennis balls were equally fluffy from use, but he needed another moment, so he returned one to the ball kid and extended his racquet for a replacement.

Out of the corner of his eye, he could see Javier tapping the side of his racquet head against the soles of his shoes—a habit borne of years practicing and playing and winning on clay.

Spencer didn't give a shit about his opponent's obvious impatience, but he didn't want a time warning on top of everything else.

His pro ranking might still be in the gutter, but that didn't make him unprofessional.

Time, Bloom.

The crowd quieted.

He positioned his left foot forty centimetres to the right of the centre mark, and half a centimetre back from the baseline.

Sometimes a millimetre was all it took to make a difference in tennis—one more millimetre forward to get the ball over the net; one more millimetre further into the court to reach for the ripping return shot.

Of course, a millimetre too far was risky too—as his unforced error stats for the first set probably showed.

He bounced his chosen ball against the hot surface of the court to warm it up, once, twice. He held it with the tips of his fingers, then rocked back and threw the ball high. It spun in a well-practiced hyperbolic arc. Just as it was about to drop, Spencer rounded his racquet behind his shoulder, shifted his left toe infinitesimally closer to the line, then swung up, over, and down across his body.

By the time the ball cleared the net, he was well and truly airborne, and, as he landed, the solid surface of the court jarred up through his left ankle, knee, and hip joints. Momentum propelled him toward the net, every muscle working in concert for the serve-volley as his kick serve ripped wide past Javier. A fast, sharp thing of beauty.

Ace!

"Foot fault!"

What!?

Spencer jerked awkwardly out of his headlong rush to the net as he whipped around to glare at the baseline umpire.

Far off to the side, his face shadowed by a baseball cap, the umpire sat with one arm stretched out, palm up, and the other relaxed with his hand set in a soft fist on his knee.

"Like hell was that a foot fault!" Spencer yelled.

The crowd collectively gasped.

A bare second later he was in the line umpire's personal space.

"Language warning, Mr. Bloom." The chair umpire's speaker-projected voice boomed around the stadium.

The line umpire tilted his head back, slow as he pleased, and Spencer sucked in a harsh breath.

Him!

"Mr Bloom!" the chair umpire bellowed again.

But Spencer couldn't move.

He couldn't think.

He couldn't do anything but lock eyes with the man who...

Who'd felt like...

Who'd tasted like...

Who'd moaned with need like...

Jesus fucking Christ. It was him. *On centre court. In...*

"Warning, Mr. Bloom."

...an umpire uniform.

Struck dumb, Spencer loomed over him with his leaden feet splayed in a 'v' shape on either side of the line umpire's shoes.

The harsh noon sun shone down on Spencer's neck, and his shadow encapsulated them in a human cave, together.

The only thing that moved was a drop of sweat that fell from his chin to the man's knee—the spatter turning that spot on his sky-blue trousers three shades darker.

"Code violation, Mr. Bloom. Intimidation."

He heard the chair umpire's words, but it was as though Spencer didn't have the power to budge. His worlds were colliding, and everything inside Spencer screamed.

Fuck!

He should have known not to indulge so close to home.

His behaviour could cost him a point, a game, possibly even the entire match. Still, he couldn't look away.

Because, that face...those lips...those rich brown eyes staring back at him.

Not harsh or demanding.

They weren't telling Spencer to get over himself.

To get his arse back in gear.

To get on with losing.

No.

They said, *breathe, Spencer.*

They said, *rest and reset in this safe space we've created.*

Spencer took a breath, and on his exhale, those eyes said, *now re-enter the fray.*

Spencer blinked.

Or, maybe he was just seeing what he wanted to see.

What he needed to see.

"Time violation, Mr. Bloom. Point to Mr. Centaurini. Love-fifteen," said the chair umpire, with a hint of steel in his voice.

"Shit." The guy—his guy—ducked his sympathetic eyes back beneath his cap, but Spencer could still see the curse on his lips.

Those lips.

The lips Spencer had attacked like a hyped-up hormonal teenager.

No finesse.

No skill.

No rhythm.

No excuse.

In that arena, he'd felt out of his depth.

But not on court.

Tennis was his home—his true safe place—where he could take charge of his body and his mind.

Spencer took a micro-step away from the stranger who'd rocked his world, and turned to face the court.

The chair umpire was right.

It *was* time.

Time to show up, Bloom. Time to show the world what you can do.

Spencer glanced across to the score board.

His start had been jittery. No doubt about that.

0-6; 0-1; 0-15

Love-six; love-one; love-fifteen.

A whole lot of zeros...a whole lotta love.

Start with nothing, Spencer.

Start at the beginning.

It was really all he could do. Because everything in his game had been off—his nerves, his rhythm, his eye for the ball.

It wasn't too dissimilar to his performance the previous night when his whole body had jittered for entirely different reasons.

He'd run away, then, embarrassed by his obvious ineptitude, scared of truly being seen.

He couldn't do that on court. Even against Javier, he had to believe he had a chance or what was the point? All he'd achieved by giving himself the grace to not win point after point—to come off second best at every turn—was certain failure.

To have any chance of winning, he had to show up and rise above expectations.

In short, he'd have to believe he could win when nobody else did.

Spencer wished he knew which way the crowd's sentiment was going.

He could feel the weight of all those bodies in the tiered stands. He doubted many of them had even heard of Spencer Bloom before they'd taken their seats, but it didn't take much for an Aussie player to reach hero status. Aussie audiences were famous for supporting the underdog. With his score card at love, he surely was that.

But what about Javier? He was a crowd favourite. The tournament directors would want him to go through. Not just to round two, but all the way to the final come Sunday.

The best Spencer could do for the whole lot of them was to put up a competitive effort.

The best he could do for himself, though, was to win.

He may be inept in the sack, but on a tennis court he had game.

All he had to do was bring it.

CHAPTER EIGHT

Spencer

The questions came thick and fast from the media scrum—leapfrogging over each other.

"Spencer! Did playing on centre court inspire you?"

"Spencer! What comes next after one of the most dramatic turnarounds in tennis history?"

"Spencer! What do you think of Anton Chalice? Are you up to a repeat performance?"

"Spencer! How did it feel to beat The Centaur?"

How did it feel?

What could he say? It felt significant.

It felt spectacular.

It felt sublime.

"Feels great, thanks."

"Spencer! What's your plan going forward?"

"A massage and a feed, most likely."

That got a few laughs.

He shifted in the seat and a million cameras flashed in his face. God knows what expression they captured. Probably him looking like he had haemorrhoids.

It wasn't the first interview he'd attended, but it was the first one where he was front and centre. After the challenge he'd conquered on court, facing the media scrum ought to have been easier, but he still felt like an imposter.

"Spencer! What fired you up?"

"Spencer! What turned the game around?"

"Spencer! Was it the foot faults?"

That made him wince, and the flashes went again.

"Spencer! Was it Garrett Fellows?"

"Ah...who?" Spencer glanced sideways to look for guidance from Kaz, his coach, standing in the wings of the media room, who oh-so-helpfully spread his hands as if to say 'I got nothing.'

Cheers, coach.

One journalist happily filled him in. "The line umpire who called you on three successive foot faults."

"Oh." *Him.*

Spencer tested out the name in his mind.

Garrett.

Garrett Fellows.

The name suited him—solid, grounded, honest—a guy you'd be happy to meet down the pub. Lovely to meet you, my good fellow. *Yeah, okay, maybe not a nineteenth-century pub.* Hey, mate. How you doing? *Better.*

"Spencer! The match turned right after the third foot fault. Do you believe in the luck of threes?"

"Spencer! Have you ever had a triple foot fault in a match before?"

"Spencer! Do you think his calls were correct?"

"Spencer! Are you going to complain to the head referee?"

"Spencer! Do believe remote ball-tracker technology should supplant line umpires here in Brisbane?"

"Spencer! Do you think the line umpire should quit?"

"Spencer! Do you think he should be fired?"

What the hell? That was wrong on so many levels. "No. Of course not."

"But, Spencer, he could have cost you the match."

Spencer glared at the journalist. "No, he wouldn't. He might've made those calls, but he wasn't the one striking the ball."

"But, Spencer—"

"No." Spencer had to squash that line of questioning. Fast. "He didn't control my foot. He wasn't the one who stepped over the line. If those foot-faults had cost me the match, which they didn't, that would've been my fault."

"But Spencer—"

"No. What I do is on me. Nobody else. Besides," Spencer stared down the persistent journalist, "it's only a game."

The media room went silent for two heartbeats, then roared back to life.

"Spencer! Is that the attitude of a champion?"

"Spencer! Do you believe you'll ever rank in the top ten?"

Their doubting questions all blurred together, till one journalist piped up with "Spencer! Would you shake hands with the man?"

Shake hands with Garrett the line umpire?

Hell, yes. In a heartbeat. That, and...

A memory of them together slammed into his mind.

...more.

What would Spencer do if he ran into the guy again? If he had another chance? Another opportunity for a kiss?

For more?

God, yes.

Except he couldn't. *They* couldn't. Spencer was a player, and Garrett was an official. The ATP code of conduct strictly forbade players and officials from having any kind of intimate relationship.

If they were discovered breaking that rule, he'd risk more than the win. He'd risk his reputation. He'd risk his ATP ranking, modest though it was. He'd possibly even risk his career.

They both would.

The way Spencer saw it, he had a choice between two opposing pathways—pursue the man, or pursue tennis.

He couldn't do both.

Yes, but Bloom, wouldn't it be worth it? To have another kiss like that. To feel consumed again like that. To...

The flood of heat to his groin brought him up short. All the journalist suggested was that he shake the man's hand. A professional touch. Nobody would call that *intimate.*

Except he knew it would be. If he ever touched Garrett Fellows again, there'd be nothing professional about it.

No chance of that, mate.

He surreptitiously put his hands in his lap.

The media scrum continued their incessant questions, but he tuned them out and gave Kaz a blunt *is it time yet?* look.

Unhelpfully, Kaz flashed his thumbs up as if to encourage him to keep speaking. To say what? Spencer didn't know, but he turned back toward the press.

"Any more questions?" he stupidly asked the room full of reporters.

When he finally escaped with Kaz back to his apartment, Spencer felt like he'd run a marathon.

"Oh, my fucking hell." Spencer's words weren't exclamatory. His adrenaline high had long gone and he had no energy left to exclaim, let alone stand upright. He threw his keys in the bowl in the entry, and leaned against the door to let Kaz through. "Tell me I never have to do that again?"

"Only if you win." Kaz thumbed Spencer's tennis bag that hung over his shoulder, "Where do you want these?"

"Don't care. Drop them wherever."

"You'll care tomorrow when you unzip it and get a wave of foot sweat up your nose."

Nice. "You're so poetic."

"I try," he preened.

It was so Kaz that Spencer had to grin. "I love you, man."

"I know. Now, go get naked and I'll throw your gear in the washing machine."

"Oh, God. Is this what it's going to be like from now on?"

"What?"

"You making inappropriate comments, and me looking around to make sure nobody overheard?"

Kaz hummed. "Probably, but you'll survive."

"What makes you say that?"

"Because you're a winner!" He sang and did an uncoordinated salsa hip swivel, shimmying down the hall to his own beat with Spencer's tennis bag for a dance partner.

Spencer pushed away from his open front door, let it swing shut, then eyed the empty corridor through the fish eye.

Where were his friends when he needed their help to escape?

Malone would be far away up north for another couple of months, yet. And Dane would still be at work obsessing over a corporate takeover, or whatever the hell he had going that week. But Lachlan and Brady would likely be around.

Brady lived life to his own nocturnal beat, and Lachlan had been secretive ever since he'd returned from his last hiking trip. But, if he called, at least one of them would come to his aid.

Probably.

"Winner!" came Kaz's off-key singing voice from deep in the apartment. "Who's a wonderful winner!"

Thud. Spencer dropped his forehead against the wood. "Ugh."

Kaz deserved to celebrate. He'd been by Spencer's side all the way through his years in the weeds. But did he have to celebrate with such Kazish enthusiasm? Could he not just sink a beer and chill?

Then again, he was sore, and Kaz did give excellent massages.

Spencer took one last look out through the fish eye, then flipped the lock and pushed away from the door. He padded down the hall to his bedroom where he toed off his tennis shoes and stripped down to all but his boxer briefs. He'd taken a quick shower before facing the media scrum, so he just flopped down on his front along the foot end of the bed.

It wasn't an ideal place for a massage, but, given the frenzy amongst players and coaches and tournament staff after he'd ousted Javier, Kaz had thought it best to avoid the treatment rooms in the player's zone. Spencer wasn't too bothered by that. Since his recent experience up close and personal with one of those massage tables wasn't exactly PG rated, it would've been awkward to be there with his coach. His luck, he'd probably spring wood the moment his skin touched leather. Better to stay away, he figured, for the moment.

Just as he was about to drift off, he heard muffled footsteps, the slap and rasp of Kaz warming his hands, then the tinkle of metal against glass.

Seconds later, warm, oiled hands landed and stroked and gouged deep into his aching muscles. Pure, blissful torture. "Mmm...so good," he purred.

"Keep up the effort and you'll get this treatment every day."

"Mmm." He could get behind that plan.

"You want the speech? Or just the massage?" Kaz asked.

"Masggrh." Spencer attempted to answer, just as Kaz's elbow dug deep into his hip flexor.

"Right, then. Speech it is."

"Nugh."

"Just think, Spencer, this tournament could be your launch button. Get through to at least the third round, and the Aussie Open would be crazy not to offer you a wildcard entry."

Spencer's breath hitched at the prospect and he lifted his face up from the bedding. "You think?"

"It depends on how other players' perform this week, but you're all so close together in points that a few wins here in Brisbane should boost your ranking by at least thirty places. Catch a good ride on the success train this summer and it's not a huge stretch to reach double figures. Maybe even top fifty. Top twenty."

"Top twelve." Spencer dared to voice. How sweet would it be to crack through to the elite players who made it onto the Champions of Tennis calendar?

Neither of them uttered the ultimate goal—number one.

Did Kaz not expect he could get there?

Did Spencer not expect it of himself?

Dare he even dream?

He may have pulled off an amazing win against The Centaur, but were the journalists right to question his competitive spirit?

Spencer's heart tripped with old, familiar doubts, questioning if he had it in him. Then a ghostly image of his brown-eyed line umpire flashed in his mind. As soon as they'd created a human cave together, calm had washed through him. What was it about Garrett Fellows whose presence could soothe, but whose touch drugged, and whose kisses made Spencer's blood rush and the world disappear?

Such different, competing, baffling desires.

Chances were, they'd cross paths on court again. The pro tennis world was small, after all. But, strangely, the thought of that didn't worry him. On court, Garrett, the umpire had proved to have a steadying effect. The real problem, as Spencer saw it, was off court—where Garrett, the man, was pure temptation.

In that arena, Spencer resolved to stay away. For both of their sakes.

Spencer dropped his face back down to the mattress and Kaz's strong thumbs ran the length of his spine from the swell of his arse to his hairline.

"Mmng," Spencer groaned.

"You can have it all, Spencer. All you have to do is stick to the plan," came Kaz's untimely reminder.

"Mfvoh."

The mother-fucking plan.

But his coach was right. For years he'd fought for the opportunity to compete against the highest echelons of tennis. If he wanted to win, he had to ignore all distractions.

Including a certain line umpire.

What if they did meet again?

In a dark, isolated, private location?

The thought alone made him shift uncomfortably on the bed—blood racing to answer that call.

"For God's sake, Spencer. Relax." Kaz pressed down hard on a pressure point.

Tingles ran down Spencer's left arm, followed by a dull ache, then a wave of bone-deep lethargy spread throughout his body, and all other concerns rushed away like the tide.

CHAPTER NINE

Garrett

Ruth stepped up onto her platform and waved over the crowd of umpires for attention. "Okay, everyone. Gather round."

God, could the day not end?

Garrett rolled his shoulders surreptitiously while Ruth rabbited on about each crew's performance that day.

He itched to get out of the whole tennis centre complex and move—a swim, a walk, ten minutes contorted over a medieval rack—anything to decompress.

It wouldn't do to advertise his weaknesses, but he'd stayed static on court for so long that it felt like every fucking muscle had seized up. When Garrett had tried to get out of his on-court seat at the end of the third match of the day, he must have looked like a decrepit old man—so stiff and sore he could barely stand upright.

Jesus, Fellows, dig yourself a grave why don't you?

He felt a nudge at his hip.

"Surviving?" Toby whispered.

"Not really," Garrett answered honestly. Toby was probably the only person he could be honest with in the officials' antechamber. Well...almost honest, he reminded himself. He couldn't tell Toby everything. "What's up?"

"Have you seen the memes?" Toby asked.

"Memes? What are you on about?"

"Of you and Bloom."

Garrett's heart tripped a beat. *Me and Spencer? What does Toby know?* He side-eyed his old friend. Was that amusement or suspicion on his face? "Me and Spencer?"

"Well, not as much him as you, but it's because of him that the meme caught on. The socials are full of you two."

Garrett pulled out his most potent ref voice. "Show me."

Toby unlocked his phone and scrolled down his feed. Dozens of posts skimmed by, all images of Garrett, taken at various angles, with his arm outstretched, palm up, like a very demanding Oliver Twist asking for more.

Whenever the feed slowed, the sound activated, and Garrett heard his ref voice call out "*foot fault*," on instant repeat, before Toby scrolled on.

"Jesus." He grabbed the phone from Toby's hand. "Are they all like that?"

"Pretty much," Toby said, not helpful at all.

"Spencer's not in them. Bloom, I mean," he shifted gears when he realised how personal he sounded, using just the man's first name.

"Keep scrolling. That's only the most recent you've seen."

How much more is there?

"Oh, hell."

Spencer's shocked face.

Spencer's annoyed face.

Spencer's resolute face.

...all with the same soundtrack, "foot fault!"

"This is..." he had no words.

"Yeah. We'll try to avoid having you two on the same court together. Luckily Ruth already had your gamma crew assigned to court three tomorrow. That'll put you well away from Bloom, who's scheduled to play the first night match."

"You're separating us?" His voice rose embarrassingly high. He ought to be glad, really, but it grated. "I *am* a professional," he protested.

But, could he be impartial? Garrett wasn't absolutely sure.

"Settle down. It's just a happy accident that you won't be on the line for his next match. After that...we'll see. Chances are he'll bow out tomorrow night and we won't have this problem anymore."

Toby's dismissal of Spencer's ability got Garrett's back up.

He wanted to protest, to point out that Spencer had it in him to win from six-love down, but he didn't, because that might have prompted more questions than he wanted to answer. Instead, Garrett asked, "Who's he playing next?"

"Anton Chalice. Bloom can move, and his height gives him an advantage, but Chalice will run him ragged. My guess is Bloom will enjoy being the hometown hero, suffer a graceful defeat, and bow out. No harm, no foul. With him out of the spotlight, this hoo-haa should all die down. Problem solved."

"Bloom's a problem now?" That didn't sit right.

"More for you than for him. The grand slam tournaments are already going toward remote ball-tracking systems, we don't need to give juice to the call that line umpires ought to be supplanted here, too. Not that I'm against technology. Can't stop progress, after all. But do you know how much those devices cost? The centre is years away from being able to buy and maintain them. Which means we need to keep the public sweet with on-court line umpires. Simple as that."

"So, you're keeping me away from Spencer Bloom purely because of the foot-fault calls?" he tested, watching Toby's face for any tell-tale hint of subterfuge. "No other reason?"

Toby's puzzled frown returned. "What other reason could there be?"

Garrett flopped back against the wall, relief warring with distaste as the truth teased the tip of his tongue.

Garrett didn't need a crystal ball to know they were each a liability for the other.

If he reported the conflict of interest between him and Spencer Bloom, he'd get a slap on the wrist and pink slip for his trouble. Not something Garrett would ever look forward to, but it wouldn't be a tragedy.

The real issue was how it would impact on Spencer.

Toby might have written him off, but Spencer still had a stake in the tournament and Garrett didn't want to stand in his way. Spencer didn't deserve to be shut out just because he unknowingly got frisky with an official.

Unless he had known who Garrett was all along.

Could Spencer have somehow known Garrett was gay, and pursued him to win favour?

Logic said no.

Garrett hadn't umpired for years. Nobody in Brisbane knew him, besides Toby. And Garrett hadn't even known which court he'd be line umpiring on till the hour before the man's match. Hell, probably even Ruth hadn't known. Also, nobody forced Garrett to trip on that fucking treadmill. No way could Spencer have engineered their meeting—with an intention to cheat, or not. To mangle Toby's phrase, the whole interlude was a happy by-product of an unhappy accident. That was all. A transgression neither of them knew they were making.

Garrett was sure of it.

He thought momentarily about seeking Spencer out for a private chat. Garrett could make it clear to the man that he had no intention of screwing him over, and they could both get on with their lives with only a minor lie hanging over each of their heads. But he wasn't sure if that plan was wise. The last time they'd been alone together neither of them had exhibited any sort of rational sense, and they'd almost been discovered. If they had true privacy, Garrett wasn't so sure that he could control himself at all. If he gave into temptation again, he'd be weighed down with an even bigger secret...and feel pressured to tell even bigger lies.

Garrett couldn't risk that. Not for his own sake. Nor for Spencer's.

"I think that's it for today. Good job, everyone." Ruth rounded up her speech. "It's been a challenge at times, but what's a tournament without a challenge, right? So, here are your assignments for tomorrow. Alpha crew..."

Since Toby had already clued him in to gamma crew's next assignment, Garrett didn't bother waiting for Ruth to finish. He shoved Toby's phone back into the man's hand with a gruff "thanks," then wove his way through the blue and taupe crowd and out into the wide central corridor.

As the heavy door closed behind him, it shut inside his last chance to own up to his lapse. The lie of omission roared loud in his mind, but Garrett had chosen his fate.

CHAPTER TEN

Spencer

Kaz woke him up from a deep sleep a few hours later to shovel down a bowl of pork balls, brown rice, broccoli, toasted nuts, and a shit-tonne of raw baby spinach, followed by a heaped bowl of banana and blueberries. If he wasn't co-matose again within an hour, it'd be a miracle. But first, Kaz insisted they discuss the game plan for his second round.

"Anton is totally different to Javier. Only the thirteenth seed. He's no Centaur. You can totally take your game to him."

Kaz was right. Anton Chalice was a serve volleyer, just like Spencer, only he was shorter, with much less of a wing span.

"Short, sharp play." Spencer summarized his game plan. Anton made up for his smaller reach with scrappiness. The man could race down just about anything on court. Spencer would have to look for tight angles and disguise his shots to have any hope of winning.

"Yes. Do what you can to close out points. Make him run, especially to his backhand, but don't expose yourself."

"Always good advice." Spencer bit into another pork ball to hide his immature smirk.

It didn't work.

Kaz gave him a withering look, then checked his phone. "Time for me to get out to the arena for Mitch's and Thomas' match. I'll see you for practice at nine tomorrow morning, as per usual. That'll give you plenty of time to rest through the afternoon. Then..."

Spencer knew how to end that sentence. "Then I bring my A game."

"That's it. This is just the beginning. You need to pace yourself." Kaz knocked the bench top. "And no more fucking foot faults!"

"Grr."

Kaz ignored his growl. "Finish up dinner, then relax. Get a good night sleep. I'll see you tomorrow morning at—"

"Nine. Got it, Coach."

But he couldn't relax. With Kaz off to coach his doubles team, Spencer floated around his apartment where there was nothing to distract him from his thoughts—all of them starring one man.

A player and an official? What they'd done together was a serious breach of the ATP code of conduct. Never mind that he hadn't known Garrett was an umpire when he'd had his tongue down the man's throat. The fact remained—he'd inappropriately...um...related with a man who was professionally out of bounds. What he'd done to Garrett in person was bad enough. What Spencer had *imagined* doing to him would...

Ugh!

Stop, Bloom.

Stop thinking.

Stop imagining.

Most of all, though, stop remembering.

Incurably restless, Spencer tried to distract himself with the view out his south-facing kitchen window where he could just see the edge of the sun dropping in the west. It burned across the sky in streaks of orange and red, and caught the high side of the tennis centre stadium that loomed across the way.

Between his apartment building and the stadium, he traced an imaginary line following the trajectory of the tunnel to the lower level of the stadium and the gym, where...

"For God's sake, Bloom." He had to stop thinking about Garrett fucking Fellows.

He needed a distraction.

Who could he call at short notice?

Not in the mood to be mocked for his idiotic libido, he skipped past Brady's contact details in his phone.

Then past Dane's. No point bothering him since he practically lived at his office twenty-four-seven.

Then Spencer landed on Lachlan's number. He might serve the purpose.

And what purpose is that, Spencer?

Distraction, of course.

From what, Spencer?

From breaking the rules for a man that I can't have.

"Fuck."

"Ha! A fine way to start a conversation, Champ." Lachlan's voice curled into his ear.

"Oh, God. Don't start that."

"What? You prefer me to call you Loser?"

"No, but..." Spencer huffed out a breath. The conversation wasn't going how he thought it would. "You free?"

"Need some distraction, eh?"

"You have no idea."

"Give me five," Lachlan said, then hung up.

"So, let me get this straight," Lachlan stilled on the weight bench, elbows locked, the vessels in his neck straining as he held the dumbbells aloft, "you did the nasty with some guy that you shouldn't have, and now you're—"

"We didn't do the nasty. We just...you know...kissed." Spencer rubbed at his mouth, but nothing could remove the ghostly memory.

It was bad enough that every place he looked around the gym reminded him of Garrett Fellows—the water fountain where Spencer had felt eyes on him, the treadmill where Garrett fell, the door to the locker room and the treatment rooms beyond where he and Garrett had been alone and...

"Earth to Spencer. Come in Spencer."

Spencer snapped back to the present. "Sorry. Not being a very good spot for you."

"Don't need spotting for dumbbells, Spence. Jeez, you call yourself an athlete."

Spencer groaned. "Don't mock."

"Are we still agonizing about the guy, or have we moved on to the match?" Lachlan asked, then released the hold and slowly lowered the weights level with his shoulders, muscles shuddering with the effort. He wasn't beefy, but he liked to keep fit—said if he ever got the crazy urge to join the armed forces, the fit-test wouldn't be the thing that stopped him.

"Against Javier?" Spencer asked.

"Nah, that's in the past, mate. I meant Anton. He's got a wicked backhand. I don't envy you."

The implied criticism about his own game rankled. "And how did you arrive at that conclusion? Been playing him lately, have you?" Spencer snapped back. Didn't he have a decent backhand? And what about his serve. Wasn't that worthy of instilling fear into his opponents?

"Be nice," Lachlan admonished. He brought the dumbbells down to waist level and sat up on the bench. "I hear what the commentators say. And the newsreaders. Not to mention all the obsessives who live with us in Tennyson Bend. All I hear is tennis, tennis, tennis."

"You don't have to live here, you know," Spencer knew he sounded pissy, and he immediately apologised. "Ugh. Sorry. Just tired of being the underdog, I guess."

Lachlan returned the dumbbells to the weights rack. "We should do this more often."

"What? You listen to me having a whinge while I do a dodgy job spotting for you in the gym?" Spencer asked.

"Funny guy. No, I just meant we should hang out more often. What with Malone off island-hopping, Dane absorbed with his merger or takeover or whatever the hell he's got going on, and

Brady being all secretive and shit, that leaves you and me to keep the home fires burning."

"Home fires?" What was Lachlan on about?

"The candle in the window," Lachlan elaborated.

Spencer tilted his head. He didn't get it.

"You know how the families of fishermen and sailors used to leave a candle in their cottage window to guide their boats home in the dark."

Spencer had no idea what Lachlan was on about. But that wasn't unusual. Lachlan wasn't off the charts intelligent, like Malone, or wildly creative, like Brady, or scary sharp, like Dane. But Lachlan had the memory of an elephant. He was their go-to-guy for pub quizzes. And Spencer was used to missing a few links in their conversations. "Whatever, man. What's next? Resistance bands? Pull ups?"

"Nah, mate. I think I'm done, but you're not."

"Not what?"

Lachlan snorted. "Not done dodging the point of our conversation."

Spencer's gaze snapped back to Lachlan. "What point?"

"You. With a mystery guy. Doing dodgy deeds."

"They weren't dodgy." Well, they were, but not in the way Lachlan meant.

"Ah-ha! So, you did do the deed." Lachlan gave a cat with the cream grin.

"Wait. What? No. We didn't *do the deed*." Why had he thought asking for Lachlan's advice would be a good idea?

"Is that the problem, then? Can't get past second base?" Lachlan waggled his eyebrows. "Or third?"

"No." *God.* "The problem is who he is. And who I am. And who we are. And—" Spencer clamped his lips shut. Lachlan was one of a small handful of people who knew he was gay. He was bursting at the seams to tell him all about his wicked interlude with Garrett, but once the truth genie was out of the bottle it'd be impossible to shove it back in.

"Well, that clears things up."

Spencer shook his head. "You don't understand."

Lachlan stared at him long enough for Spencer's eye to get twitchy.

He pitied the poor students Lachlan taught—none of those kids stood a chance against his bullshit detector.

"Y'know, Spence, I reckon I know you pretty well."

That was true. "Better than most."

"Exactly. I'm above average in the 'who knows Spencer best' ranks."

"If there ever was such a thing. Sure."

"But that doesn't mean I can read your mind."

Thank God for that.

Spencer did a three-sixty of the gym. Mostly to get Lachlan's far-too-insightful gaze off of him, but also to check the gym for anyone close enough to overhear their conversation. All was quiet, and it seemed like they were alone, but the gym wasn't one big, open room. It had nooks and crannies where anyone could be lurking.

He felt hyper exposed—and not just by the harsh, fluorescent strip lights that buzzed in the ceiling. He itched to get outside. Fresh air, fresh ideas, fresh perspective.

The desperate thought gave him a great idea. "Let's go for a dawn run out at Toohey Forest tomorrow."

"On a match day?" Lachlan's voice betrayed his surprise.

"Shit." Lachlan was right. No way would Kaz be happy if he took off like that. Too big a risk before his next match. But Spencer needed a place of safety—a space where he could spill his secrets to a trusted friend. "I'm not due to play till the evening session."

"Yeah, but...this is your chance, Spence. Whatever you've got going with this guy can't be important enough to screw with your future."

Meaning Lachlan thought he was screwing it up.

"I know," Spencer agreed. But he couldn't let it go.

Something about the situation with Garrett felt momentous. Meaningful. He knew it sounded ridiculous, but it wasn't in him to give up so easily. Besides, screwing up his connection to Garrett felt like the greater risk. "I go for a run every morning. Going to Toohey Forest would just be shifting the location. I'll be back in time for practice."

Lachlan raised an eyebrow.

Ugh. He should have known Lachlan would make him do the sensible thing. "Fine. But next time I need advice, I'm calling Brady."

"Look. It's totally legit to be wound up after today. No shame in being a bit nervous, or whatever's got your knickers in a twist. But there are easier, far less risky ways to find perspective than running around in rough bushland at fucking four a.m. in the morning. C'mon. Let's get out of here." Lachlan grabbed his towel from the weight bench, hooked his left elbow around

Spencer's neck, and propelled them toward the door. "I need a shower, and you need your beauty rest."

"Ugh. No way can I sleep." All he'd do was stew.

"Win or lose. Just strive to do your best. Isn't that what Kaz says?"

"I know." Neither of them was wrong, which made admitting it that much more annoying.

"Give it a day. If you lose tomorrow night, Kaz won't care so much if you sprain an ankle leaping around on those bloody rocks."

"It's called bouldering."

"Whatever. The point stands. Toohey Forest can wait till you've lost a round."

"Gee, thanks. Way to be supportive."

Lachlan shrugged. "Just sayin'. Toohey Forest can wait."

Someone swung the gym's main door open.

"I know. It's just—" Spencer stopped dead in his tracks.

He'd recognise that visage anywhere.

Garrett Fellows.

"Fuck." Spencer pulled up, catching Lachlan off-guard.

"What's wrong?"

"It's him."

"Him who?"

"*Him!*"

"Him...? Oh, *Him*!"

Shit! "Quick! Do something." Spencer dipped to try to get out from Lachlan's arm, but his friend only cinched him in tighter.

Garrett's gaze skipped between him and Lachlan, who was giving off way-more-than-friends vibes. Which really wasn't the impression Spencer wanted to give.

Sure. Garrett was out of bounds, but Spencer didn't want him to think that Lachlan was his boyfriend, or that he'd messed about behind anyone's back. That wasn't Spencer's style.

If he could just speak to the man. Properly. Without risk that anyone would see or overhear them together. He had no idea what he wanted to say, but he had to say *something*. Because, even though they couldn't repeat it, the last thing Spencer wanted Garrett to think was that he regretted it.

Nothing could be further from the truth.

Spencer hip-checked Lachlan, then in an overly loud, over the top voice, said, "So, yeah, I reckon a dawn run Wednesday morning in Toohey Forest sounds great. Before the summer heat kicks in. Pity you can't make it, Lachy, since your boyfriend likes to get cosy first thing, eh?" He nudged Lachlan in the kidney with his elbow, sharp, and ducked out from under his friend's arm.

"Ow!" Lachlan turned his mocking gaze on Spencer.

Spencer glared at his friend in return and tried to communicate telepathically how important it was that Lachlan didn't fuck up his moment. He wanted to speak to Garrett. He wanted to explain what happened. He wanted to make sure the guy knew that while they could never, ever cross that boundary again, it wasn't because he didn't think the guy was gorgeous, or worthy, or any other fucking thing that came under the banner that read—*I want you.*

Lachlan's mouth did the guppy thing, then he came out with, "Sure...ah...yeah...a real pity. You know how I love getting up for a run at the arse crack of dawn. Pity my boyfriend...um...Darcy...needs my attention right then. Or I'd help you out with my...friendly company. Right, mate?"

Darcy? This isn't a fucking Jane Austen novel. This is real life.

"Yeah." Spencer cleared his throat. "Exactly. Such a shame that nobody else is keen to get out there with me. And it's only, like, a ten-minute drive from here. Easy. Just roll out of bed and you're practically there. Right?"

"Right," Lachlan agreed. "Except for the sex."

Spencer blinked. "What sex?"

Lachlan's eyebrows climbed. "The very satisfying sex at the arse crack of dawn that my oh-so-fabulous boyfriend Darcy and I will be having at the exact same moment that you'll be out at Toohey Forest, all alone, which isn't all that safe, considering the wildlife out there—snakes, you know, and...koalas, and...yeah, anyway...and wishing you had company...except you don't, so..." He ran out of words.

Which was a very, very, *very* good thing.

Face flaming, Spencer turned back to Garrett.

Had Garrett received Lachlan's so-not-subtle message? Spencer couldn't tell. The man was pursing his lips. It wasn't quite a pucker, but Spencer could imagine how with a bit of a nibble, it'd be easy to persuade them to soften, and open, and...

Garrett's lips softened, and opened, and...said, "You need protection? From snakes and...koalas?" His scepticism was clear.

Spencer wasn't quite sure how to answer that. Koalas never hurt anyone, and snakes had never bothered him. But if a fake fear of snakes was what would get Garrett to meet him out there, then, "Yes."

Absolutely, yes.

Garrett held his stare, then gave a swift nod. And, Spencer had to fight a smile as he responded in kind.

"Okey-dokey, then." Lachlan clapped his hands, breaking the spell.

Garrett's intent gaze fell away and he rapped his knuckles against the open door beside him. "Any chance I can get past you guys and into the gym? I've got a date with a treadmill."

God, no. Not the treadmill.

"Sure, yeah. Sorry, mate." Lachlan unhooked from Spencer's neck, stepped aside, and swept his arm wide like the ringmaster at a circus, "Have at it."

"Awesome. Thanks."

Spencer tracked Garrett as he passed between them.

Garrett got a few steps in, then stopped, turned, and held his hand out to Lachlan to shake. "Lachy, is it?"

"Lachlan." Lachlan re-closed the gap between himself and Spencer. "Only Spence gets to call me Lachy."

"Spence. Right." Garrett's eyes shifted to Spencer for a bare half second, then he shook Lachlan's hand. "I'm Garrett. Good to meet you."

"Likewise."

Garrett spared a hint of a glance for Spencer, then headed off to the wall of cardio machines.

Spencer couldn't be sure, but he thought the man walked with a bit of a limp.

He wanted to ask Garrett if he was alright.

He wanted to ask if his face was alright.

In fact, he wanted to ask a lot of things, including...

"Coming?" Lachlan interrupted Spencer's swirling thoughts.

"What? Oh, yeah. Sorry."

In silence, Spencer followed Lachlan out of the gym and into the corridor, through the connecting security door, along the tunnel to their Tennyson Bend basement, up the elevator to level six, and down the hall to Spencer's apartment. It wasn't until his front door snicked shut that Lachlan spoke.

"Alrighty then. Spill."

CHAPTER ELEVEN

Garrett

The giant stadium night lights lit up the blue court and reflected along the white lines of the field of play. Garrett sat so high up, he must have resembled a blur from the court, and the chance that anyone would recognise him was pretty damn low, but he curled the peak of his cap tighter around his temples, anyway. After those memes had spread far and wide, he wouldn't put it past some tennis-mad junkie in the audience to spot him, or for the roving television cameras to throw his face up onto the arena screen for all the world to see.

They called the cheap seats the gods for a reason. From the spare seat he'd found in the highest row of the stands, the stadium was laid out for him like the Roman Coliseum, where, way down below, Spencer Bloom and Anton Chalice fought like gladiators.

Spencer looked as dishevelled as ever. His sweaty shirt was rucked up at the back, exposing a triangle of skin, and half his hair looked like it had escaped his man bun. He repeatedly shoved it out of his eyes and back behind his ears, but it didn't stay.

He wondered why Spencer wasn't wearing one of those headbands all the tennis legends wore back in the seventies, back when Jesus hair was a thing.

Unless growing his hair long was one of his ticks. Maybe it was a symbol of some kind.

In Garrett's experience, sports people often had odd habits and superstitions. For all he knew, Spencer might believe he was doomed to lose if he didn't lace up his left shoe first, or wear his briefs inside out, or collect his not-quite-long-enough hair up into a man bun. Garrett didn't know. He didn't know much about the man at all—unlike the two guys who knew Spencer well enough to have a spot in his player's box.

Garrett knew who one of them was—Lachlan, Spencer's overly familiar, touchy-feely friend. The other guy, who Garrett figured was probably his coach, sported steel-grey hair and skin like tanned leather.

From his distant perch up in the stands, Garrett couldn't see their expressions, but their body language shouted *We support you, Spencer Bloom!* They looked like they wanted to leap out onto the court and go into battle for their boy.

He knew it was irrational, but the sight irritated Garrett no end. He wanted to be down there—to be free to openly support his guy through every point, every win, and every loss.

His guy?

Jesus, Garrett. Get a grip.

Spencer Bloom isn't your guy.

He studiously returned his attention to the court where his eyes gravitated back to Spencer—to flicker from the concave hollows behind his knees, to the pronounced bone at his wrist, to the triangle of sweat-sheened skin visible at his collar.

Garrett couldn't help it. He needed to gather all the details to sift through later.

Spencer was striking more than he was gorgeous. Sharp-featured. Lean. Like he needed to beef up his roast potato intake. Having been up close and personal on two separate occasions, though, Garrett knew there was more than skin and bone to grab onto. Beneath all that height, the man was physically strong.

But mentally?

That, Garrett wasn't so sure about.

Anton Chalice was the clear favourite to win.

With his scrappy style of play, Chalice had pushed Spencer all over the court, taking the first set in a handy fashion. But not everything had gone the thirteenth-seed's way. In the second set, Spencer was holding his own at three games apiece.

The crowd chanted for Spencer—clearly hoping their newly-discovered local hero would do them proud.

Garrett didn't cheer. He didn't clap or yell or whistle. He didn't do any of that for Anton. Or for Spencer. Not outwardly.

On the outside, he did his best to remain calm, professional, mute.

On the inside, though, adrenaline surged through his veins for Spencer.

Garrett had forgotten what it was like—the see-saw of tennis—of how one minute the game, set, match would be going in one competitor's favour, and then the next it'd shift. All it took was one winning shot, one ace, one solid return, one baseline out-manoeuvre, one skilful slice, one lucky nick of the net, one wrong hit, one long shot, one mistimed volley, one foot fault...to turn the whole game around.

Shit. Just the memory of those foot faults had his hand clenching around the hard edges of his plastic seat.

At thirty-all, Anton ripped a slice serve out so wide that it ought to have been a winner, but Spencer's height gave him the wingspan of a vulture. At full-stretch he flicked his wrist and snapped a cracker forehand down the ad line.

"Thirty-forty." Came the chair umpire's call.

Break point.

The giant screen lit up with a spinning tennis ball icon. The crowd hollered, "Bloom!" and "Winner!" and "C'mon!", urging Spencer to keep running, keep reaching, keep winning.

Garrett squeezed the plastic seat harder.

It didn't hurt.

Much.

Come on, Spencer!

The seventh game of any set was critical—a psychological boon. If Spencer could break Chalice and take the game, then the match would still be an uphill battle but he'd be a major step closer to the win.

Don't get ahead of yourself, Garrett.

One shot at a time.

One point at a time.

Win or lose.

That was how simple sport was. Each moment a simple binary.

Ones and zeros.

Black and white.

Except watching Spencer didn't feel that way.

Each moment felt red—like bright arterial blood pulsing, rushing, sending bright sparks to the edges of his vision.

Garrett's attention yo-yoed from the distant action on court to the magnified action on the big screen.

Spencer's grey shirt had turned three shades darker, every inch of skin shone, and his white tennis shorts looked weighted down from his own personal waterfall of sweat.

He looked good.

Despite being down a set in the match, Spencer's round-one victory had given him confidence, and it showed.

His stride had lengthened, his hips rolled with greater ease, and his reactions had stepped up a gear.

Anton had a decent serve, but it wasn't as big or as fast as some, and Spencer took up an assertive position half a foot behind the line at the back corner of the deuce court. Legs splayed wide, he slicked sweat from his brow with his left pointer finger, tapped the surface of the court once with his racquet head, then found his grip and squatted. Poised to receive.

The whole dance sang to Garrett.

Which was fucking ridiculous.

He ought to be focused on the game. Not on some guy who kissed like a desperate mess and played tennis like he had nothing to lose.

Spencer crossed to the ad court, stepped right up onto the baseline, slicked his stray locks back, splayed his legs, tapped the court with his racquet, gripped the racquet handle with both hands, then lifted his head and stared his opponent down.

Chalice danced on the line, then tossed the ball and swung through.

"Fault!" called the sideline umpire.

Spencer moved forward a foot inside the baseline to receive the second serve.

Jesus, Spencer. Give yourself space to see the ball.

But it wasn't in Spencer's style of play to give an inch. No way would he step back from the brink to appease the laws of physics, the gods of sport, or Garrett's stress limits.

Garrett wriggled his toes, rolled his shoulders, and dug his thumbs into the insertion points of his quads to each knee.

When it came to his injuries, being still was like sitting on a landmine.

The trick was to stay loose and limber, and he'd learned early on in his recovery to shift and flex and breathe through the discomfort. But he'd never been all that good about wilfully relaxing, and the tension of watching Spencer play was putting that weakness to the test.

"Sorry," Garrett muttered to the woman sitting to his right when he accidentally elbowed her.

"No worries. Small seats, eh?"

That was putting it mildly.

Chalice took an extra moment to compose himself at the service line. He rolled his neck and bounced the ball more than usual, stalling for time. Then he tossed, swung, hit through, and raced to the net.

A bouncer straight up the T.

Spencer stretched to get his backhand on it.

"Fault!" called the line umpire.

Long! Spencer breaks!

Anton pulled up. He glared at the centre service line, then swung to face the umpire. "The hell that was out!" His shout so loud it clearly was audible at the top of the stands.

Garrett shot a quick glance at the electronic scoreboard.

Reviews Remaining:

Anton Chalice – 0

Spencer Bloom – 2

The crowd roared.

The chair umpire reached for his microphone, but Spencer held his hand up to interrupt and touched his toe to the centre service line.

The crowd was so loud that Garrett couldn't hear what was going on, but the two guys in Spencer's player's box sure could. They shot up as if their seats were sparked by live-wires.

The chair umpire pushed the microphone and his tablet aside and leaned forward as Spencer and Anton both approached the chair, till all three were together in a tight huddle.

Garrett stood and stretched up onto his tippy toes, needing to see and hear and know whatever the hell was going on.

The crowd hooted and whistled. Sensing blood.

Twenty seconds went by...both players gesticulating wildly.

Thirty.

Then the three separated and the chair umpire announced, "Mr. Chalice and Mr. Bloom will replay the point. Mr. Chalice to serve."

What the hell! He gave up a break? Is Spencer Bloom for real?

Honest sportsmanship was one thing, but Garrett had never heard of anyone doing that. Was he truly that honest?

Fairness was one thing, but who does that?

Nobody.

Ever.

Even the most sporting soul took advantage of the rules to win.

At least, that was Garrett's experience.

He felt a tiny band of cynicism melt from around his heart.

"Thirty-Forty. Second serve. Mr. Chalice. Your serve."

The crowd stomped wildly—a herd of rabid beasts.

Garrett stilled—the eye of the storm—all his attention focused on Spencer.

Seemingly calm, Spencer jogged back to the ad court baseline and repeated his dance—hair slicked, legs splayed, court tapped, racquet gripped...ready to receive.

"Quiet, please," called the chair umpire.

At the other end, Anton bounced the ball at least a dozen times. Then stopped and backed a step off the line.

On the big screen, Garrett could see the tension in his shoulders.

The service clock ticked down.

Four seconds.

Three seconds.

Two...

Chalice stepped up to the baseline, bounced the ball once, twice, then served a safe, loping bouncer.

Spencer had no trouble getting racquet to ball, and they set into trading baseline shots.

Anton conservatively stayed well inside the lines.

Spencer pushed the boundaries.

When Anton sent a ball short in the court, Spencer sliced deep into his backhand, then charged to the net, feet wide across the centre line, racquet poised for anything.

But Spencer must not have disguised his intention well enough because Anton caught the ball early and sent it in a surprise lob high into the glare of the stadium lights.

The crowd responded in one collective gasp as the tiny yellow ball arced high over Spencer's head.

Garrett didn't watch the ball. He watched Spencer.

Quick! He wanted to yell. *Run!*

But Spencer didn't run.

He didn't scrap for the ball.

Not like Chalice would have done.

Pure instinct, he dug in his heels and crouched deep—a coiled spring—and launched high. Right arm stretched to full capacity, he just managed to connect. The ball hit the frame of his racquet and shot off so fast Garrett could barely track its trajectory. Like a pinball, it deflected sideways, skimmed just over the net, half the court away from where Chalice stood, flat-footed. It ricocheted off the hard blue surface, into the air, straight into the hands of the chair umpire.

The crowd collectively gasped.

Then hushed.

Then...

"Game, Mr. Bloom."

And the crowd went wild.

CHAPTER TWELVE

Spencer

Would Garrett come?

The chance that he would take Spencer up on his oh-so-subtle, *not*, hint to join him for a run at Toohey Forest was slim to none.

Just roll out of bed and you're practically there.

Holy shit. Could he be any more of a dork?

His previous twenty-four hours hadn't been too shabby on the human-success index—what with his fucking awesome win over Anton Chalice. In thirty-six hours, he'd have to be back on court, prepared to prove himself all over again. But that challenge felt like nothing compared to the will he/won't he questions that cluttered Spencer's mind.

When he usually came to the bushland preserve for a dawn run, he'd follow the seven-kilometre undulating circuit that trailed through the forest to skim past the university campus and back. But what if Garrett did show up? That trail would put him well out of sight.

So, instead, Spencer stuck close to the entrance and repeated the much shorter Sandstone circuit once, twice, three times. He kept an eye out, ducking his head every time he passed hikers and runners and climbers and sleep-deprived parents with wide-eyed babies strapped to their chests, just in case someone might recognise him, but he saw no sign of Garrett.

The blanched dawn light sharpened as the sun slowly rose above the horizon, shooting streaks of white gold through the gum trees—the promise of a hot day ahead. By the time he jogged the final leg on his sixth loop and closed in on the short track that would lead him out of the bush to the carpark, Spencer had pretty much given up.

No sign of Garrett meant the man felt nothing for him. No interest. No connection.

Right?

It was a relief, he told himself.

The last thing he needed was a distraction when he was finally forging success on court.

But there, at the final junction of the circuit, decked out in a well-loved t-shirt, loose, low-slung jeans, and scuffed sneakers, was Garrett.

The breath Spencer didn't even know he'd been holding in huffed out.

God. What was it about the man? He was like a yoga class and a HIIT session all rolled into one—Spencer felt simultaneously revved up and calmed down, and his attention zeroed in. He couldn't look away.

Garrett must have heard his footfalls on the rough path because he looked up. "Hey." He uncrossed his arms from his chest and shifted away from the wooden track sign where he'd perched his arse.

Spencer dropped out of his jog. "Hey." *Brilliant, Spencer. Repeat everything the man says, why don't you?* "You made it."

Garrett nodded.

They stared at each other for God knows how long, accompanied by the scrunch of sticks and stones beneath their feet, the rising chatter of sun-loving cicadas, and the cacophony of birds greeting the day.

Then Garrett asked, "You been for a run already?" Which was also so fucking not smooth that Spencer had to smile.

"Yeah. I was just about done. But we could run another circuit if you like." Which was a stupid thing to suggest. The man was wearing jeans, for fuck's sake. No way had he come planning to run.

But he *had* come.

Why was he there then?

"Nah. That's okay." Garrett hooked his thumbs through his jean loops. "Looks like you could do with a cool down though. How about a walk?"

Spencer had barely broken a sweat jogging the track, let alone anything requiring a dedicated cool down. But if Garrett wanted to walk...

"Sure. I could do a walk. Let's go this way. You'll get a better view of the sandstone boulders." Garrett fell in beside him and he started back up the rough path for the seventh time that morning.

After a few steps he had to modify his pace.

Garrett's limp was back.

Not super-pronounced, but Spencer was used to watching how people moved—it came second-nature to note an opponent's physical weakness.

Not that Garrett was an opponent.

He was...

Spencer didn't know what he was.

A hook up?

Not entirely.

An ally?

Possibly.

A person of interest?

Well...

Garrett was a person...and every fibre of Spencer's being sure was interested. But the phrase made it sound like they were in a fucking police procedural, and he seriously doubted Garrett was a murderer luring him into the bush to kill him.

For one thing, he'd been the one to do the luring.

Again.

Jesus. How the fuck had he leaped so fast from the man having a limp, to him being a mass murderer?

Spencer shook off the ridiculous thought.

Garrett wasn't dodgy. He was an umpire. Nobody got to the position he was in without proving he or she was an upstanding citizen.

Except he broke the rules to come and meet me here.

That choice didn't exactly scream upstanding citizen.

Are you any better, Spencer Bloom?

Well, I know I'm not a fucking mass murderer.

He bit his lower lip. "So..."

"So…" Garrett said at the same time.

Spencer snorted. "We ought to record audio of this conversation and sell it. Make a mint."

"Scintillating," Garrett concurred, straight-faced.

Spencer grinned. "That's one word for it."

"Enchanting."

"Um. If you say so." He was enchanted, but the general population might not find it…

"Captivating."

"Oh, now, let's not get too carried away." The thought of being Garrett's captive was a smidge too close to Spencer's earlier fancy. The man was *not* luring him to his death. He was ninety-nine-point-nine-nine percent sure of it.

"Dazzling," Garrett went on.

"Did you swallow the thesaurus, or something?"

"Or something."

"Ha! Droll. I like it."

I like you.

Spencer couldn't ignore it anymore. He had a crush. He'd entered crush city. Hell, he'd practically claimed the gold-plated key from the mayor.

Spencer slowed his pace to taffy speed—not wanting their walk together to end.

"You like sarcasm?" Garrett asked.

"You sound surprised."

"Sarcasm is a twisting of the truth." Garrett shrugged. "I just thought…the way you gave up that point last night. Even the fairest sportsperson is rarely one-hundred-percent honest. It was…something."

It only took half a second for Spencer to realise what Garrett was talking about.

Strictly speaking, he hadn't given up the point. He'd given Anton the chance to replay a point that should have continued. But that wasn't the detail that caught Spencer's attention. "You watched my match last night? Were you there?"

Garrett shoved his hands into his back pockets. The move bulked his pecs and biceps and tightened his t-shirt across his chest. The man wasn't built. He was no athlete. But Spencer could tell there was strength there—a tension-filled wiriness.

Look away, Bloom.

"Staff get bonus seats," Garrett said.

"Ah." Freebies. No particular wish to see him play, then. "Of course."

Spencer wanted to ask him what he thought of his win, but crossing that line would acknowledge that he was a player, and Garrett was an umpire, and that by meeting at all, let alone in secret, they were both putting their heads on the chopping block.

Knowingly.

Again.

Even more than that, opening himself up for the man's critique felt like tearing open his ribcage and exposing his heart. Garrett hadn't said anything negative, but Spencer's success in the tournament felt so tenuous. He didn't know if he could take it.

Not yet.

He started a mental list of all the things they shouldn't talk about:

Tennis.

The truth.

He ran out.

What else was there?

Jesus. Was his life really that pathetic?

It was like being on the most painful date on the planet.

If it even was a date...

Ugh!

What was safe for them to talk about?

Spencer looked around and latched onto the thing glaring them in the face.

"Rocks."

"Huh?"

"Boulders." He pointed up the hill to the massive sandstone boulders that littered the landscape. He'd call them the devil's marbles if there wasn't already a place in the Aussie Outback with that name. "I'm pretty sure they got left here during the last ice age. Glacier moraine." He pointed up the slope again like the dorkiest of tourist guides. "Maybe. I'm not actually sure about that. But it sounds plausible, doesn't it?"

Garrett blinked.

For a micro-second, Spencer wished Lachlan was there. He'd know all about how the landscape was formed. Then he doused that thought. He did he want Lachlan intruding on his private time with Garrett.

Hell, no.

"Come on." Spencer snagged the hem of Garrett's t-shirt.

Normally, he'd leap off the path and stride cross-country up to his favourite boulder, but he had to remember the way

Garrett walked. Something physical was going on for the guy. Some kind of injury, or disability, or...Spencer wasn't sure what. He could ask, but...yeah, no. He was used to talking about his own body. It was integral to his job. He might be used to it, but that didn't mean he liked it. Or approved. He usually wanted to tell Kaz or his mother or whoever else to piss off. They didn't have an intrinsic right to his body.

Nobody did.

And Garrett deserved the same right to privacy.

If he wanted to tell Spencer what made him limp, he could. But Spencer vowed not to press for answers.

He gave a quick tilt of his head up the gentle switch-back path, and repeated. "It's not too far to the ridge-top platform. A couple hundred metres at most. You can see the biggest boulders from there."

Nothing in life was eternal, but he wanted to put his hands to the rocks. The feel of their aged solidity made him feel young and alive. If it wasn't cheesy, he'd call them his touchstones. And he wanted to share them with Garrett.

Just as he and Garrett arrived at the outlook platform, an older couple left, leaving them alone.

Together.

They stood silent for so long, staring out through the sparse eucalyptus bushland, that Spencer's mind started to feel like a pressure cooker.

Out of the blue, Garrett asked, "Did I read you wrong?"

"Huh?"

"Back in the gym? Your..." Garrett seemed to struggle for the right word. "Interest," he said, then gave a breathy chuckle.

"That seems a woefully inadequate word to describe the mad scramble we made of each other."

"Oh." The pressure cooker in Spencer's head blew. "No. I mean, yes. I mean, no you didn't read me wrong. Yes, I want you here. Yes, I'm interested. It's just..."

Garrett looked back up. "Do I make you nervous?"

"A bit," he confessed.

Garrett took a step back.

"Wait. No." He reached out to Garrett's arm to stop him. "I don't mean like that. It's just that by coming here, we're breaking every single rule in the book. And I..."

Garrett winced. "Not every single rule. There's a few that we're not..."

"Okay, so maybe not *every* single rule. But that's not really why I'm nervous." Could he be honest with Garrett? His only basis of trust was gut instinct, and that said 'yes'.

"Then why?" Garrett asked.

God. He was going to make Spencer admit it.

He hoped the man appreciated cheesiness. "I feel weirdly connected to you. Drawn to you. In a non-creepy, non-Siamese-twin sort of way," he rushed to reassure Garrett. "I promise."

Garrett moved closer. "Drawn to me?"

"Mm-hmm." Spencer couldn't explain it. He just knew with every molecule that he was in the right place, with the right person, feeling the right thing. When he was near Garrett, he felt a heady mix of passion and comfort. It was intense, and Spencer didn't want it to end.

"Like a magnet?" Garrett asked.

"Ugh. Sure. I guess 'magnet' works. In a totally non-cheesy—"

"Non-creepy, non-Siamese-twin sort of way." Garrett nodded with a straight face. "Agreed."

Spencer sighed with stupid relief.

Down the slope of the ridgeline, a couple of climbers cheered as they scaled the top of a boulder. Arms around each other, they celebrated their shared win—their synchronicity. Spencer couldn't help but smile. "Wanna try it?" he asked.

"Try what?"

Spencer jerked his head in the direction of the climbers. "Bouldering."

Garrett snorted. "Win the Aussie Open. Buy me a bionic body. And then, maybe, I'll give it a try."

Win the Australian Open? Hell, yes. He liked that predicted future. And he wasn't at all disappointed that Garrett didn't want to join the strangers. Besides, he had a different kind of bouldering in mind.

Spencer stepped down from the wooden platform onto the scrubby sea of rocks, then turned. "Think you can handle a rocky path?" He held his right hand out.

Would Garrett take it?

Yes!

"Where are we going?" Garrett asked.

Spencer tilted his head back and to the right. "Over there."

"What's over there?"

"Rocks."

"So funny."

Garrett's grip was strong, but his fingers weren't callused like Spencer's. He didn't spend hours every day gripping leather, resisting the friction of hard-hit balls. Not that Spencer had much of an idea of what Garrett did on a daily basis. He barely knew the guy at all.

Not that that seemed to matter.

He led Garrett away from the climbers, down the rough, rocky slope, past the first over-hanging boulder where visitors would still be able to see them, and wove through the trees toward his favourite.

"Where are we going?" Garrett asked.

"Don't want to tempt fate by getting caught together."

"We'll both be screwed if we're found out."

"Exactly."

"If you're so worried about it, why even suggest we meet today?"

Spencer thought about that for a long moment, but he didn't have a good answer—a rational answer—so he stayed silent as he picked the easiest path through the familiar jumble of rocks and crackling dead-fall that littered the forest floor.

Before too long, they descended to the lower face of his favourite boulder. A massive, rectangular block of sandstone, twenty paces across, and twice Spencer's height. It sat heavy between young, scrubby eucalyptus and patches of wattle. The ground in front of the lower face was flat-packed dirt, making it easy for Garrett to traverse, but Spencer didn't let his hand go.

When it felt like life was ripping along too fast, the boulders at Toohey Forest were one of his favourite places to just go and be. Against them, he felt tiny. Insignificant. A fleeting speck in time and space.

No matter what he did, how well he played, how high he scaled the ranks of success, the boulders gave him perspective. They helped him see that the universe would cope whether he won a title or not.

Life would go on.

A small, wishful voice in his minded added—just as life would go on if he and Garrett were caught together.

He trailed his free hand along the jagged, crystalline surface of the boulder to the centre where he knew they were unlikely to be seen from any direction. Then he turned, backed up against the middle of it, and spread his stance to bring his height down a few inches. He wanted to see Garrett's every expression straight on.

No hiding.

Garrett's lips twitch. Amused.

"Something funny?" Spencer asked.

"No. Yes."

"Well, that's clear." Spencer echoed Garrett's words. "What then?"

"I can see you thinking."

"Oh? What am I thinking about?" Spencer tried to school his expression, but when the barest tip of Garrett's tongue flicked out the corner of his mouth, he completely lost track of why. The jagged surface of the rock scraped his shoulder blades as he inhaled. It might have even cut through his shirt to his skin, but he didn't care.

"You're thinking about that night." Garrett stepped closer.

Spencer hadn't been thinking about it, but he knew instantly what Garrett meant. *That* night.

The night they'd met.

The night they'd touched for the first time.

He let Garrett's hand go and slid his palm up the man's forearm, the crisp hairs lightning strikes to his senses. The rougher knob of his elbow proved the man had a few years on him—probably a few more than his own twenty-four—but Spencer wasn't put off by it. Warm palm on cool skin, his hand rounded the man's upper arm and teased his fingers up under Garrett's thin t-shirt sleeve.

Spencer repeated the move with his left hand. His thumb burrowing higher till he felt a hint of pit hair.

Garrett huffed a laugh.

"Ticklish?"

"No. Not particularly." Garrett smiled a secret smile, then shuffled close enough that it wasn't just their heights in alignment.

The pleased rumble from Garrett's throat seemed to vibrate the air between them. Then he said, "Is that a rock I feel, or are you just pleased to see me?"

Distracted by the sensory cocktail, it took a second or three for Spencer's mind to make sense of the words.

"Oh my God." He knocked his top knot back against the rock and looked up to the pale early morning sky. Glorious private time in nature, and the sexy devil wanted to spoil it with corny jokes? Seriously? "Are all the men around here comedians?"

Garrett rotated to look left and then right—teasingly causing their chests to brush together. "I don't see any other men."

To give as good as he got, Spencer lifted up onto the balls of his feet and made a show of peering down the ridge to the right to where he could hear the other pair's distant chatter and clangs of metal on stone. "Good thing."

"Hey." Garrett gripped his chin and brought him back down to earth. "I'm right here."

The rock scraped against his back, but Spencer barely felt it. Their breaths combined, and he couldn't hold back any longer. He captured Garrett's bottom lip between his teeth, then dove in for a taste.

CHAPTER THIRTEEN

Garrett

The way Spencer kissed him wasn't smooth. He had no tactics. His frantic mouth was all teeth and tongue and shuddering breath.

Garrett would have told him to slow down. He *should* have told him to slow down. To stop. To think. To beware the volcano that could erupt under both of their careers if they continued. But Spencer's clumsy urgency lit something deep in Garrett's core. It told him that Spencer had no more control over the attraction between them than he did.

As though neither of them had the power to hold back.

As though every touch was necessary.

As though *they* were necessary.

And all the reasons not to touch flew away as Garrett responded with his whole body.

He hooked his fingers under Spencer's firm arse, stubbed his toes up against the boulder to get as close as humanly possible, and sandwiched Spencer between the sandstone boulder and his own rock-hard cock. Locked together, he couldn't even find a moment to unzip his jeans. He ignored the twinge down his right leg and ground into Spencer, instinct finding a rhythm that had them both groaning.

Spencer never stopped touching him. He'd claimed he wasn't the caveman type, but the earthiness of their surrounds seemed to unleash something in him and his hands seemed to be everywhere—stroking, pressing, pulling, pushing—for all the strength and callused roughness of his grip, he had a sensual touch that set every one of Garrett's nerve endings firing.

Never letting up on the desperate grind, Garrett pulled his mouth away from Spencer's kiss to suck in a much-needed breath. He trailed his lips across to the corner of Spencer's jaw, then down to feel the thrum of his pulse.

Spencer stretched his neck, offering, and Garrett gladly took. He nipped and licked his way to the soft skin beneath Spencer's ear where he inhaled the salty-sweet scent of the man. "Need you naked." He tugged on his fleshy earlobe.

Spencer shuddered. "Uh...yeah...yes."

But they couldn't.

Not there.

PDA was one thing; charges of indecent exposure another.

Garrett didn't lift Spencer's shirt like he wanted to.

He didn't grope under the waistband of Spencer's shorts and wrap his hand around Spencer's cock.

He didn't shove Spencer's shorts down and slide his fingers down Spencer's crack to the waiting heat inside.

He didn't do any of those things.

Garrett ignored the twinge in his back and the strain in his leg. He held them together in a messy, writhing frott that seemed to go on, and on, that had his nerves firing and balls tightening—desperate for release.

"Need," Spencer panted into his ear.

"Yeah."

"You."

"Yeah." So close. He was so, so close.

"Need you."

Heat bloomed at the base of Garrett's spine. He couldn't get a word out to warn Spencer, but his body spoke volumes. He gripped underneath Spencer's arse cheeks and thrust him rougher into the boulder.

With one hand anchored to the back of Garrett's neck, and the other clawing at his ribs, Spencer squeezed his eyes shut and clenched his jaw, like he was fighting something rabid within.

The sight set Garrett off and he bit down on Spencer's shoulder to try to stop his cry of sweet agony as his hips stuttered and his balls finally surrendered their load in his jeans in a hot sticky mess.

"Oh, my fucking hell!" Garrett hadn't come like that since he was a randy teenager in heat. He leaned into Spencer, his breath catching on each spasm that rippled through his body, and on the heels of his orgasm came a wave of blissful lethargy.

Needing another taste, he scoured his lips against Spencer's scruffy cheek in search of the soft warmth of his lips. If his body had been up to it, Garrett would've gone down on his knees. Right then and there. He would have taken Spencer in his mouth to taste his essence.

Failing that, he explored Spencer's mouth, feeling the taut frenulum on the slick underside of his tongue and the sandpaper roughness above. Spencer whimpered, breathless, as Garrett sucked the meat of it into the heat of his own mouth and ground his hips against the younger man's hardness in a slow, agonizing, insistent beat. He felt Spencer's fingertips claw at his back, but Garrett didn't let up and it wasn't long before Spencer's head jerked back and Garrett felt against his belly the electric pulse of Spencer's rod as he, too, came.

"Ah! Fuck!" Spencer shout rang out.

Garrett had just enough wit left to pull his hand from where it gripped Spencer's arse cheek and slapped it over the man's mouth. "Shh."

"Fugh," Spencer repeated, quieter, muffled by Garrett's hand.

"Shhh." He repeated. If someone heard them, they'd both be up shit creek. He ought to have been worried for himself, but all he could think to do was cover Spencer—to protect him from view.

They stayed like that, nearly still but for their heaving breaths, till the sounds of the bush encroached once more.

Garrett groaned anew when a kookaburra started up—the bird's insane laughter far too late to cloak Spencer's cry.

"Where's a cone of silence when you need one?" Garrett asked the universe. "Or an invisibility cloak?" Because, Jesus, if anyone had seen them—never mind shit creek, they'd be front page news.

Another kookaburra joined the melee and Garrett wondered briefly if he ought to feel performance anxiety.

"What the hell was that?" Spencer asked.

Garrett tilted his head back to see Spencer's expression properly. From the look of his glazed eyes and flush-streaked cheeks, Garrett didn't think he was asking about the bloody birds. "You need me to tell you what that was?"

"No. No. Not that." He blushed even harder. "I meant this…" Spencer wavered a hand in the narrow space between them, "insanity."

"Ah." He meant the extraordinary chemistry between them. "God knows."

All Garrett knew was he'd lost control.

Hell, he'd even lost time.

Sometime during their descent into Neanderthal mode, the sun had arced at least ten degrees higher, throwing nature's spotlight directly onto Spencer's face. Not that Spencer needed to be lit for Garrett to notice him.

Ugh. Sappy much, Fellows.

"So…" Spencer bit his lip.

Suddenly, the afterglow evaporated and all of Garrett's aches and pains roared back to life. Was Spencer about to run again? "So?" he asked, pressing the question.

"What are we going to do now?" Spencer asked.

"We?" Garrett felt something inside him soften. *Does Spencer feel the same sentiment that I feel?*

A furrow appeared between Spencer's brows. "Unless you don't think we're stuck in this together."

"Together—yes. Stuck—no." Garrett objected to the inference that they weren't both free to make their own decisions, or their own mistakes. He'd come to Toohey Forest of his own volition. As had Spencer.

Unable to not touch, Garrett slid a hand under the hem of Spencer's shirt and skimmed up the side of his ribs, seeking a response. "We can stop," he said, not entirely sure that he spoke the truth, "This can stop."

Spencer's nostrils flared.

Garrett smoothed his hand higher, seeking the crinkle of Spencer's chest hair. "You want to pretend it never happened? Go back to life as normal." Garrett wasn't about to force him into anything. But Spencer was the first thing that had felt right since the day of his accident. Damn the rule book—he wasn't giving that up without a fight.

He skimmed the pad of his thumb across Spencer's nipple. It puckered and Garrett gave it a little pinch of approval.

"Stop that. I can't think."

With his other hand, Garrett tilted Spencer's chin down, as if seeking a kiss, then diverted sideways to brush his cheek across Spencer's scruff to his ear, where he broke his own rule to always champion the truth, and whispered, "I can keep a secret. Can you?"

A heavy hush descended over the forest, and Garrett's breath stopped, until he heard...

"Hell, yes."

Chapter Fourteen

Spencer

"This isn't the most embarrassing walk of shame I've ever taken, but it sure as hell is the most adventurous." Garrett grimaced. "And the most uncomfortable."

"Agreed." Spencer could only imagine how Garrett was feeling in his restrictive jeans.

He leaped up onto the wooden platform and tried his best to discreetly pull the silky material of his running shorts from his cum-plastered cock and balls. He really needed a shower.

"Delicately done." Garrett muttered behind him.

Spencer turned to find the man still down on the rocks, staring at his arse.

"Like what you see?"

Garrett snorted at his transparent grab for attention. "More like what I'm about to see."

"About to...? Oh! That sounds promising."

Garrett stiffly leveraged himself up with a grunt.

It was obvious Garrett was feeling discomfort. And Spencer supposed he ought to feel guilty for going off-track. But he couldn't bring himself to regret any part of their time together.

"So, I guess that's a no to bouldering?" Spencer was only half joking.

Garrett looked back over his shoulder to where the couple with the ropes and the clanking carabiners had just climbed to the top of another giant boulder. "Maybe next century."

"But this century has barely begun," Spencer jokingly protested. Having a legit reason to scramble around in the wild with Garrett sounded like a great idea to him. He couldn't help but be disappointed that Garrett wasn't up to the challenge.

Garrett shook his right leg, rearranged the front of his jeans, then retreated off the platform to the edge of the path where he turned back around and quirked his lip. "Coming?"

"And you call me the droll one." Spencer mock-grumbled as he again matched pace with Garrett's step. "Shower?"

"God, yes."

"Breakfast?" He pushed for more.

"Sure. Just have to get to the tennis centre by ten."

"And I have practice at nine." Spencer glanced at his watch and grinned when he saw it wasn't even six o'clock yet. Plenty of time. So, he made his final offer. "Me?"

"Ha!" Garrett didn't answer with a yes, or a no, but Spencer didn't need a verbal response—not from the way he felt Garrett's hot gaze trail up his body, or how the proprietary hand pressed at the small of his back.

That touch lifted him to ridiculously giddy heights.

Spencer wanted to reach out and touch, too. He wanted to hook his thumb into the back loop of Garrett's jeans and claim ownership.

But he didn't.

He didn't touch Garrett then.

Or all the way along the remainder of the circuit to his car.

Or on the drive back to Tennyson Bend.

Or in the building's basement carpark.

Or in the elevator up to level six.

Or all the way along the corridor to his apartment door.

On the inside, though...

The door lock had barely snicked shut when the true tussle began.

"My turn." Just as Garrett had done to him up against the boulder, Spencer rounded on him, pressed him up against the back of the door, and claimed his mouth.

"Oof."

Teeth and tongues and hot breath.

"Mmm. You taste so good." Earthy and sweet. He sucked on Garrett's tongue, then delved deep in search of more.

Garrett's fingers scoured his back, and pushed his t-shirt up so high it yanked at his armpits. "Off," he grunted into Spencer's mouth.

To comply, Spencer would have to step away, and he didn't want to do that.

But Garrett was a bossy arsehole.

From behind, he curled his hands around and over Spencer's shoulders and tugged him a bare inch back, just far enough to break their lip lock. "Shower."

"Okay, okay. Geez. Talk about one track mind." The tease came out muffled as Garrett gripped the material of Spencer's t-shirt and yanked it up and over his head. "Ouch!"

"Sorry. Didn't mean to catch your man bun." Garrett's hands returned to Spencer's scalp to soothe the hair that'd practically been ripped from their follicles.

"I told you, it's not a man bun. It's a—"

"Knot or a club, yeah. I remember."

"Are you mocking my hair? Because people who mock my hair don't stay on my good side."

"Oh, really? What happens to people who get on your bad side?"

"Well..." His mind went blank.

Shit.

"Do you skewer them?" Garrett asked with a hip thrust.

It was cheesy and ridiculous, but that didn't stop Spencer's blood from rushing to his groin. "Depends."

"Do you knock them over the head with your club and drag them back to your cave?"

"You've got a thing for cavemen, don't you?"

"Would you rather I tease you about knotting?"

Knotting? "Umm." He was confused. "What?"

Garrett chuckled. "Oh, man. You really have lived a tunnel-vision life. I need to select a few choice novels for you to read."

Novels? "What the hell does reading have to do with my hair?"

"Nothing." Garrett gathered the loose strands that hung loose from his temple and shoved them behind Spencer's ear. "Nothing at all."

"Well, then..." Spencer was at a loss.

It wasn't as though he had a whole lot of experience seducing men, but the moment wasn't how he'd imagined it would go with Garrett. Clearly, he needed to do something drastic to get things back on track. None of that cheesy, joking around bullshit. He needed to be sexy—bring some kind of game to the mix.

He stuck his tongue back in Garrett's mouth.

It seemed to do the job, so he kept up the lip-lock as he shuffle-waltzed Garrett through his apartment, down the hall to his bedroom, and into his ensuite bathroom. While he did that, he multitasked by kicking off his shoes and shedding the remainder of his clothes.

Then he went to work on Garrett's jeans.

He got them un-buttoned and an inch down before Garrett slapped a restraining hand to his own thigh. "I have...scars. They're not a nice sight."

"Really? Are they as gruesome as mine?" He twisted to show the three puckered scars around his left shoulder, each about the diameter of a ten-cent piece. "Look like gunshot wounds, don't they? In through the front, out through the back? Except there's three." He flashed three fingers. "Doesn't really add up."

Garrett touched the one in the front with his fingertip, then played dot-to-dot with the other two. "What happened?"

"Rotator cuff. I had key-hole surgery, but the joint got infected. Had to go back for a washout. The whole disaster took me out of action for nearly a year, and I still don't have full movement on that side." He rolled it, and felt the familiar tug of things not being quite right. "Good thing I'm not a leftie, eh?"

"But your backhand's great."

It warmed Spencer's heart to hear Garrett had noticed. "It isn't as good now as it was. But it serves me okay."

"Jesus." Garrett stroked lightly down Spencer's bare arm.

He shivered at the touch, but Spencer didn't move away.

"It's funny, isn't it?" Garrett's voice had turned gravel rough, as though borne from rocks formed millennia ago.

"Funny?" There was nothing funny-ha-ha about his injury, but Spencer had a feeling Garrett hadn't meant that.

"How a single moment..." Garrett paused, and his gazed dropped to track his hand as his fingertips skimmed back up to Spencer's shoulder. There, he found the three scars and pressed. "How one single moment can split your life in two vastly different directions. One tiny little thing. One decision. One event. One simple shift in circumstances. And everything changes."

Oh, he knew that feeling well. "A fork in the road."

"Exactly. Do you ever wonder..." Garrett's words petered out.

Ah, the 'what if?' game. He'd played that too—far too many times.

"Life takes funny turns sometimes," Garrett said. "Take that night, for instance."

"What night?"

The world went a bit fuzzy as Garrett shifted his hand from Spencer's shoulder to cup Spencer's neck and comb his fingers up into his hair. Against the grain. It was exactly the same move Garrett had made in the treatment room right before they'd—*Oh!*

That night.

Talk about forks in the road.

He'd learned long ago not to worry about what could have been about paths not taken. What mattered most was to identify the best shot in the moment, and to go for it.

Spencer kept his voice light as he asked, "What about your scars? I showed you mine..."

Garrett rolled his eyes. "I'll show you mine if you show me yours? Is that the bargain?"

"Technically, I already did show you mine. But, yeah...sounds fair to me." Spencer turned to reach for the shower tap. What Spencer wanted was Garrett—all of Garrett, naked and wet, scars and all. But if the prospect of skin-on-skin wasn't enough of an appeal, perhaps the comfort of a hot shower would do the trick.

He heard a rustle, and a quick glance in the bathroom mirror revealed skin. A whole lot of skin. And a host of pink, barely healed scars.

"Holy shit." Spencer wished the words back the moment they left his mouth.

Garrett stilled with his shirt tangled in his arms above his head, then he turned to face Spencer. He slowly dropped his shirt to the floor, toed off his shoes, and shucked his jeans all the way off.

It was a test, Spencer knew.

He was good at tests. Good at reading the play. Good at trusting his reflexes. Good at going after what he wanted.

Spencer didn't wait another second. He stepped right up into Garrett's personal space and placed his hand flat in the centre of his chest.

He felt the rise and fall of Garrett's breath.

Inhale, exhale.

He flared his fingers to thread through the whirls of Garrett's crisp brown hair.

Inhale, exhale.

He called to mind the feeling of absolute rightness he'd felt in Toohey Forest when pressed between the lifeless rock and Garrett's passionate intensity. He'd felt a driving need to touch and taste and practically inhabit Garrett's skin.

He wanted that feeling again—to embrace honest desire and animal instinct.

He wanted to lose himself in sensation.

Spencer leaned into the man and breathed deep. "Can you smell it?"

"What?" Garrett's word came out gravel rough.

Spencer buried his nose in the short waves at Garrett's temple, and inhaled their combined desire—both the old and the new. "Us."

The rumble of Garrett's groan vibrated through the palm of his flared hand.

"What do you want?" Garrett asked.

God. So much. I want so much. But, to begin...

"I want to taste you." Not giving the man further cause to think, Spencer led Garrett into the steamy shower and proceeded to taste every part of him, starting with his scars.

CHAPTER FIFTEEN

Spencer

Holy hellishly God, Garrett was like gasoline thrown into the fire of Spencer's libido, and he hadn't even made it to the man's front yet.

Spencer's shower was a generous size, but he'd crowded Garrett in and wrapped his arms around his front to touch and feel whatever he could get to—ostensibly to help wash away the sticky jizz, but Garrett had seen straight through that tactic.

They'd fallen into a teasing game of 'cop a feel' that ended with Garrett leaning on his forearms against the steam-slick wall tiles, Spencer on his knees with his hands gripped like starfish to the meat of Garrett's wide-braced thighs, and Spencer's tongue lashing at the pucker of Garrett's hole.

It was sordid and wild and goddamn heavenly.

The hot spray pelted Garrett's neck and shoulders, turning his summer-gold skin peach-pink. Rivulets coiled between his just-visible ribs, into the slight indent above his hips, and down his crack.

"Too much." Garrett groaned, at the same time as he leaned over a little deeper, and stuck his arse out encouragingly.

The mixed message didn't sway Spencer from his goal. He'd long ago learned to look past signs of deception to a player's core movement, and Garrett had most definitely shifted his centre of gravity at least an inch toward Spencer.

Or, more accurately, toward Spencer's hungry mouth.

The man wanted it.

Bad.

He gave Garrett's quivering thighs another squeeze in acknowledgement, then followed a wayward trail of water over the crest of Garrett's firm arse cheek to a light birth mark shaped, curiously, like a peach. He nipped at it gently before slowly sliding the tip of his tongue down to the crease at the top of Garrett's thigh, and across to the man's centre.

Like a fucking homing beacon.

Garrett shuddered. "For fuck's sake, Spence. Either get to the good bit, or I'll come."

"Patience," Spencer ignored Garrett's gruff threat. He was having too much fun learning Garrett's body, feeling his rhythms, observing his subtle tells, to rush anything. His mind sparked with all the plays he could make—the shots they could trade—before he went in for the kill.

The hairs on Garrett's thighs crinkled against his callused palms as he ran them down and around and up between his legs to softly cup Garrett's balls with one hand, and pressed the other hand to the small of his back, gently, but insistently, till Garrett was practically bent in half.

God. What a sight.

He wanted to see through Garrett's eyes too—to see down Garrett's taut abdomen, past his untamed bush where his heavy cock speared the air, dripping shower water and viscous pre-come. Further on, framed between his thighs and Spencer's wide-spread knees, Garrett would see Spencer's hard cock, throbbing, angry, desperate to be inside his tight heat.

Fuck! Just the thought of it had Spencer ready to shoot.

He clamped his fingers around the base of his cock and gave Garrett's hole the spear of his tongue instead.

"Aargh, fuck!" Garrett gasped. "Do that again."

"Bossy."

"Horny," Garrett countered.

Answering that call, Spencer speared his tongue in, once...twice...triggering sensitive nerves, then flattened his tongue to rest there a moment and feel the involuntary pulses of Garrett's muscular ring.

Spencer ran the tip of his tongue along Garrett's taint, following the line down the centre of his wrinkled sac, and pressed into the groove between his marble-hard...

Garrett moaned.

Spencer replaced his tongue with his index finger and pulsed teasingly between Garrett's balls. Then he swiped his tongue back up Garrett's taint to again tease his pucker with nips and licks and the rough of his scruffy chin, never letting up while Garrett squirmed and moaned and cursed.

"Uhng!"

A hand tangled in his hair and tugged.

"Condom. Lube," Garrett ground out.

"In that order?" Spencer snickered, enjoying the tease. He wasn't done tasting, but preparation wasn't a bad idea. Garrett was so hot, there was a very real risk Spencer would lose his head well before they got anywhere close to actual fucking.

He gave Garrett's balls one more loving squeeze, kissed his right arse cheek, then rose up off of his knees and chased the steam out of the shower as he opened the glass door and traipsed, dripping wet, to his bedside table.

The lube was an easy grab, but, "Condoms, condoms...grr! Where are you?" He shuffled through all the crap he'd accumulated, finally finding a crumpled box in his bottom draw with a few remaining foil squares inside. "Jesus, fuck. Please be okay." He gave one of them a quick check over. "Thank you, God."

By the time he got back to the shower, Garrett had taken matters into his own hand.

Spencer plastered himself to Garrett's back, bit the muscle at the side of his neck that tensed with every rhythmic jerk, and ran his fingers down Garrett's flexing arm to drag his hand away.

"Mine," Spencer said, and pinned Garrett's renegade wrist to the tile wall.

"Hurry up, then." Came Garrett's rough grumble of displeasure at the interruption.

"Cheeky." He brushed his scruff up over Garrett's sharp jawline and took his lips in a deep, angled kiss, swallowing whatever other demands Garrett might think to make.

It was tempting to stay right there. His cock had already aligned to Garrett's crack—his throbbing vein rubbing at Garrett's hole. It'd be so easy to line up and press inside. But Spencer had a game plan, and he wouldn't be diverted.

He broke their drugging kiss and mouthed his way down
Garrett's spine. Faster that time.

On target.

He manhandled Garrett back into the position he'd left him,
hips perfectly angled for Spencer to re-commence his attack.

Spencer didn't usually get into rimming guys. It was too
personal. More personal than fucking, for sure. But something
about Garrett make Spencer want to dive in deep. To fill his
senses with nothing but Garrett. Spencer wanted to feel him,
smell him, taste him—to know him in all the ways.

He held each arse cheek with a star-fished hand, thumbs to
either side of Garrett's hole, and spread him wide enough to give
Spencer open season.

Water ran in rivulets over the quivering hole that opened
and shut like a hungry maw in chorus with Garrett's moans
and impatient curses. Spencer blew on it, sending shivers and
a ripple of goose bumps across Garrett's bare skin. Soon, he
promised himself, he'd taste each and every one of them, but
neither he nor Garrett could wait that long.

Not that time.

He pulsed his thumbs into Garrett's tender flesh. Not slow.
But not fast, either. A nagging rhythm that had Garrett pushing
back toward him and Spencer's hips rolling, thrusting into the
steamy air, both of them searching for more.

"Spence." Garrett's voice was gravel over rock. Needy.

Giving in, he leaned in and touched the flat of his tongue to
Garrett's hole. There, he closed his eyes for a second, relishing
the wild race of his beating heart and the answering call of
Garrett's pulse at his core.

The sound of the shower rushed around them, containing Garrett's cries as Spencer firmed his tongue and finally dove in.

CHAPTER SIXTEEN

Garrett

Still damp from the shower, Garrett shoved Spencer's comforter aside and collapsed onto his back.

The mattress was a Posturepedic wet dream, and all Garrett wanted to do was wallow in the afterglow of the best orgasm he'd had in months. Maybe even years.

From the rumpled bed, he watched Spencer do a rough dry of his long hair. "I like it when you go all caveman on me" Garrett said.

"When did I go caveman this time?"

"When you dragged me back to your cave and had your wicked way with me."

"Wicked, huh?"

"Very wicked. Downright dirty."

Spencer stiffened a fraction. "Dirty good? Or, dirty bad?"

"Oh, dirty very, very good." Just the memory of it had Garrett's cock stirring all over again.

If anyone had ever told Garrett he could orgasm from a rim job, he'd have told them they we're dreaming. He just wasn't that sensitive.

Maybe it was because, before Spencer, he'd not been touched for so long. Not in *that* way.

He'd had plenty of doctors and nurses and therapists put their hands on him. But they weren't Spencer.

And they hadn't used their tongue.

"I'll reciprocate," he promised, "As soon as I get muscle function back."

Spencer snorted, threw his towel in the direction of his bathroom, then kneeled on the side of the bed.

Garrett watched him prowl the few feet separating them, plaster his front to Garrett's left side, then stretch his ridiculously long legs out to dangle half-on, half-off the end of the bed.

"Comfy?" Garrett asked as he curled his arm around Spencer's broad shoulders.

Spencer didn't answer, but his rumble of satisfaction vibrated right through Garrett's ribs till he swore he could feel it in his spleen.

Spencer playfully traced a spiral on Garrett's chest, coiling tighter and tighter till he got to the centre, then stopped. It wasn't exactly over Garrett's heart, but the touch made him feel again like he was the subject of Spencer's intense focus—the centre of Spencer's world.

It was intoxicating.

"D'you feel okay?" Spencer asked. "Did I exhaust you?"

Garrett ran his body through a quick status update. A few twinges here and there, but, given the acrobatics of the previous hour, he was feeling all kinds of fine. The word *sated* came to mind. "Very okay. But I'll need a breather before the next round."

"Shame. I was going to suggest we fuck like bunnies till I get it right. But if you're exhausted..." Spencer trailed off.

Garrett ran his thumb over the cusp of Spencer's left shoulder. "You looking for a score in this arena too?"

"Ooh," Spencer looked delighted, "that never occurred to me. Yes, please. What's my rating now?"

Garrett held up his first finger. *Numero uno.*

Spencer grabbed it. "Too easy. I need specific parameters for success. We need a post-orgasm scoring system."

"No. What we need is a post-orgasm sleeping system." Garrett wrestled his finger from Spencer's grip, then twisted to grab his whole hand and wove their fingers together.

Garrett shut his eyes and did his best to think calm, restful, restorative thoughts.

It was difficult when he had an arm full of hot-as-hell man.

"But, how will I know what I have to do to improve?" Spencer asked.

"Shh. Rest."

"But..."

Garrett sighed. "You don't need to do anything to improve."

"So, you're saying it was perfect—that I was perfect?" Spencer sounded like he was teasing, but from his stillness, Garrett could tell that his answer was important.

Was Spencer having performance anxiety? Surely not.

"There is no perfect or imperfect when it comes to sex."

Spencer was silent for a long beat. "Ignoring for a moment the fact that that sounds like a challenge, what is there then?"

Garrett half shrugged. "Release. Pleasure." With someone as intent on achieving his goals as Spencer, those were definite.

"Well, I know that, but still..."

"Adoration. Intimacy."

Spencer's scruff tickled Garrett's chest as he nodded without lifting his head. "I could go for those."

Garrett skimmed his left hand the length of Spencer's warm back. His skin was so smooth—silk over strength.

"Love?" Spencer ventured into the extended silence.

"Ah." Garrett hadn't intended to go that far. "Advanced level stuff."

"Hmm...so sex is kind of the opposite to tennis."

Garrett tried, but he couldn't figure out what Spencer meant. "How do you figure?"

Spencer shifted back up onto his elbow. "In this game," he released Garrett's fingers and waved his hand over the two of them twined together in bed, "love does not equal zero."

Garrett blinked. "Ahh..."

"Too much?" Spencer gave a little smirk.

"Tiny bit."

Spencer lay back down on Garrett's chest. "Yeah. Thought so."

Except it wasn't.

Not really.

Spencer wove his fingers into Garrett's chest hair and gave a little tug. "This is nice."

In his heart, Garrett agreed. It really was.

Everything they'd done together felt nice.

And worth way more than zero.

Spencer in his arms felt so real. So right. But it was a bubble that would eventually have to burst. One way or another, the world would come crashing in.

"Do umpires get rated too? I never thought to ask."

"Not in the same way, because we don't compete against each other, but sure."

"How did you get into it?"

"Refereeing?"

"Refereeing, umpiring, officiating. All of the above."

"Sports psych."

"Really?" Spencer twisted his face to lean his chin on Garrett's chest.

"Yeah. Wasn't to be, though. I fell into officiating during the last year of my degree, and never went back to uni. My dad still gives me grief over that."

"What, you tripped and fell into an umpire's seat?"

"Nah, nothing like that. It was a field-research project. I decided to go on the road for the summer semester and ref for every sport I could think of. Any tournament at the local, regional, even state level, though it was hard to crack into that at first. My dad runs a regional tennis comp that I'd helped out at for years, so I was already qualified to officiate for tennis, but that summer we found tournaments and trials for swimming, athletics, triathlon, field hockey, basketball, volleyball, even lawn bowls. The weirdest sport was a penny-farthing race in this tiny town down in Tasmania. Crazy place."

"We?"

"Toby and I. We were doing the same university course."

"Ah. Toby." Spencer fished, giving Garrett a tiny thrill at the man's evident jealousy.

Garrett smoothed his hand over the puckered scars on Spencer's shoulder, then reached with his other hand to press a finger to the little frown between his eyebrows. It was cute, but Spencer had no reason to worry. "Didn't last. We'd chucked it in before the semester was even over. I'd found my passion for refereeing. He had not. End of story."

"Hmm." Spencer bit at his lower lip. "Tennis does have a way of sucking people in."

"God, no. Not tennis. Sorry. There's nothing wrong with tennis, but that's not the sport that got me hooked."

"What then?"

"Footy."

"Aussie Rules football? Seriously?"

Was that judgement he heard in Spencer's voice? Garrett stiffened. He wasn't usually defensive about his choice of career, but the loss of it still felt as raw as it had the day of the accident. "Seriously."

"That explains why we've never crossed paths before."

It took Garrett a second to recognise Spencer's words as innocuous, and to lay down his hackles.

Spencer stared at him for a moment through slitted eyes, then he said, "I can see you out there on a footy oval. Are you the guy who starts play in the middle of the field, who throws in from the side, who signals a goal, or, who runs around in the mud handing out red cards to all those hooligan footballers when they act up? Or, some other ref thing? Is there anything else? Please say you run around in the muddy muck. That'd be so much fun."

"All of the above," he answered.

"Hmm." Spencer idly pulled at a single hair in the middle of his chest. "You must be pretty damn fit to ref those footy matches. Ninety minutes, aren't they? Something like that."

"Twenty-minute quarters, plus time on. Could be anywhere up to about two hours."

"Exactly. You must run, like, a half marathon per game. Maybe more."

"Some games." Not any more, though.

"You're an athlete," Spencer said.

"Was." He *was* an athlete. Past tense. Not that the physical challenge was ever the biggest source of reward for him. "What I really miss is being keyed into the game. A footy match is a logistical mess of mud and testosterone and the ticking clock. My job was to keep focus amongst the chaos. The thing about refereeing is that it's not all that much about the sport. I mean, it is—you have to understand the rules, and regulations, and the rhythm of whatever sporting code you're working in—but it's mostly about making fair and precise split-second decisions while adrenaline buzzes through your system."

"You love it," Spencer said. It wasn't a question.

"Yeah." The word came out as barely a breath. "It's gutting to think *never again*. Not for a pro game. Not since the accident."

"You were injured that bad? Career ending?"

"Yeah." It was all he could get out.

"Oh, man. I'm sorry. That seriously sucks."

It really did. "I'm fully functional—"

"I can attest to that." Spencer waggled his eyebrows.

It shouldn't have been cute.

Garrett tsk'd. More at his own idiocy for falling into the trap than at Spencer. "Fully functional," he repeated in a firmer voice, "But the AFL medical panel won't clear me to return. An insurance thing, they said. Apparently being more metal than bone makes employing me too high a risk."

"Idiots," was all Spencer had to say to that. Enough to give Garrett a warm rush of comfort.

He shook himself. "Enough about my fucked-up life. What about you? You said your shoulder surgery took you out of tennis for a year. Did you ever think about quitting? Shifting gears?"

"God, yes. Many times."

"But you stuck with it. You did make it back." For a second, Garrett expected bitterness to creep in at Spencer's burgeoning success. But it gave him hope. If anything, it needed protecting. Which meant he ought to get out of the man's way.

We should stop this. We should stop this now. He tested the words in his mind, but he couldn't bring himself to say them out loud.

Searching for a diversion, Garrett played with the ends of Spencer's damp locks. "I feel like there must be a story here. What's with the Jesus hair?"

"You don't like it?"

"I like it fine." He wove his fingers deeper into it and demonstrated just how fine he liked it by guiding Spencer up for a lingering kiss. "Mmm. See."

"Mmm." Spencer snuggled back down on his chest, but Garrett didn't let go of the man's hair. He felt inordinately proprietary about it.

"I'll cut it eventually. Hopefully. Someday. Maybe. I will."

That was a convoluted mess of possibility. "You will?"

"Mm-hmm. Soon as I win a pro title." Spencer brushed his lips oh-so-gently against Garrett's nipple. It was almost distracting enough to take his attention away from Spencer's words.

Almost.

"That's..." *Wow*. Spencer had incredible talent, but the cynic in Garrett wondered if anyone had ever told him he could be waiting forever for that to eventuate. "How long have you been growing it for?"

"Not long. Three years, plus a bit. Since my shoulder recovered and I returned to the circuit." Spencer gave the ends a tussle, flicked them back over his shoulder, then returned his hand to Garrett's chest where he seemed to think it ought to belong. "My sister, Casey, thinks I should shave it all off and donate it to charity. She calls it my loser hair."

"Loser hair? That's seriously fucked up. What did you tell her?"

"I said I've gotten attached." He snorted. "Literally."

Garrett reached across with his right hand and tucked a stray lock behind Spencer's ear.

The wayward strand bounced straight back out.

"You ought to wear one of those headbands that were cool back in the seventies. Keep it off your face."

"I tried one, but it gave me a headache. Same with baseball caps."

"Head too big?" Garrett ran his finger across the width of Spencer's forehead.

"Ha! Not that head." Spencer winked.

Garrett groaned. "So, you plan to cut it off when you win?" He let his right arm fall back on the sheet beside him.

"D'know. Don't get me wrong. I'd love to win a major title. Prove I can do it. Hold that shiny trophy up for the world to see." He raised his fist in the air, then dropped it and snagged the very same lock of hair that Garrett had tried to smooth back. He stretched it taut, as high in the air as it would go. Then he let it go. "But after a while you realise how much the little wins matter. It's hard to cut off something that represents persistence and determination."

"Courage, too."

"Sure. Some of that."

"Takes masses of courage to put yourself out there the way you do. I admire the way you go for it."

Spencer shrugged. "Not as much as I used to. I'm far more cautious now. More patient. I don't think I could ever go back to being that rash player who leaped at absolutely everything, regardless of the potential payoff. Being taken out of action like that forced me to change my ways. I had to re-learn what to expect of myself." He shrugged, as if that was nothing, but Garrett could hear the resolve in his voice. "I used the time to train as a coach, and, as soon as I could hold a racquet without hurting myself, I started working with juniors and adult novices. It was good. Turns out I enjoy helping people discover who they are as players. It's probably what I'll end up doing after I retire, but..."

Oh, to be able to pick and choose when to retire from a sporting career he loved. Garrett swallowed that bitter pill, then completed Spencer's sentence with a gruff, "Not yet."

Spencer nodded his agreement. "Anyway, when I got the Player in Residence gig and moved from my college dorm to Tennyson Bend, I met a bunch of guys who all live and play here."

"Pros?" Or, was Spencer about to tell him about some other guys he fooled around with? Garrett's mind flinched at the thought of anyone else touching him.

"No. They're just regular guys who enjoy hitting the ball around. At first, when they invited me to play tennis with them, I figured they were angling for free coaching. But no. Half the time they relegate me to ball-boy duty. They don't care who I am. They don't give a shit that I can serve at two-hundred k's per hour, with an average of eighty-three-point-six percent first serves in."

"Accuracy is important."

"Sure, during tournaments it is, but not between friends. With them, I can make all the dunce shots I like. It's..."

"Liberating?" The freedom to take his eye off the ball wasn't something Garrett ever craved, but it made sense for Spencer to appreciate it. "Mistakes must feel like a luxury to someone who competes for a living."

"Exactly. I'd love it if every day was like that. But there are things I want to achieve first."

"Such as a legit cut of your loser hair?" Garrett asked.

"Ha! Yes. Although the hair is just a symbol of my goal. I keep it because I like it. It'll be a wrench to cut it off when I win...if I ever win."

"When," Garrett asserted. He made a show of eyeing the messy mop of hair. "You'd look a whole lot less sexy without your man bun."

Spencer growled as he flopped his forehead down on Garrett, "It's not a fucking man bun."

Garrett did his best to ignore how the half-dried locks coiled with his chest hair like vines clinging to wire. "And you'd be a whole lot less top heavy. Which would be a real shame. I like you toppy."

"Grr." Spencer raised his head again and glared. "I'm trying to make a serious point here."

"And that is?" Garrett asked, struggling to keep a straight face. Spencer was so damn cute.

Spencer's glare drifted to look out the window. Or maybe into his own thoughts. "Shit. I forgot." A frown line appeared between his brows. "Damn you for distracting me."

"Distracting you? All I'm doing is lying here."

"Exactly. Lying here, looking all gorgeous and shit."

"You're the one plastered to me." Garrett pointed out. If anyone had a right to complain about gorgeous distractions, it was him.

He flared his fingers wide and distracted them both by combing up from Spencer's hairline at the back of his neck to his crown, then sifted out through the burnished-gold lengths—through the evidence of Spencer's grit and determination.

Spencer sighed and butterfly-kissed Garretts pec with his nose. "Mmm...so good."

Mimicking Garrett's motion, he followed the groove of Garrett's sternum to run his fingernails up through the curls on Garrett's chest.

Right then, Garrett Fellows knew he'd fallen twelve-point-five percent in love with Spencer Bloom—a good one-eighth of him was hook-line-and-sinkered.

It wasn't the original plan, but it was done.

He released Spencer's hair and stretched both arms out wide, hoping the cool of the sheets would shock some sense into him. But the move drew his shoulder blades together and raised his chest infinitesimally closer to Spencer's warm hand. It woke something up in him, and Garrett didn't think he could stay away.

Giving in, Garrett let his body relax. He sunk deeper into the comforting bed, and curled his arm around Spencer's shoulders.

He'd have to depend on the remaining eighty-seven-point-five percent of his rational self to remind him that what he and Spencer had was temporary. He wouldn't be in Brisbane for much longer, and Spencer's star was rising fast. Spencer was moving up, while Garrett was doing his level best not to knock himself out on the way down.

"Want someone along for the ride?" The words just slipped out. Garrett squeezed his eyes shut and tried to hide from his own idiocy.

Why did he have to screw up a perfectly friendly post-sex chat with romantic bullshit like that? The problem was he'd been a thorny briar for so long that one hit of happy had his heart lit up like a neon rainbow.

He was about to speak up—take it back; laugh it off—but then Spencer said, "Yeah. Yeah, I do." And his warm hand flattened in the middle of Garrett's chest.

Claimed.

Garrett covered it with his own to hold it in place. "For real?"

"Yeah."

Spencer's short answer seemed certain, but what was he certain about? Garrett needed to know exactly what he was getting into. "Together? In public?"

"Oh...ah...well, no, that's not what I..." Spencer cleared his throat, and the hand under Garrett's twitched, like a butterfly desperate to flutter away. "I'm not out."

He wasn't in the business of outing anyone, but Spencer's rejection still stung. He shifted his torso a fraction of an inch away from the man's warmth, which twisted his lumbar spine, which sent a hot streak of pain down his right leg.

He stilled, cold sweat peaked on his upper lip, and he held his breath to ride out the tremor that followed.

Jesus. How could he be so stupid?

"Hey. You're okay. Breathe." Garrett heard Spencer's voice through the rushing sound in his ears.

Inexplicably, he felt Spencer close the gap between them.

Spencer should have felt heavy where he settled over the left side of Garrett's chest. But, instead, it felt grounding to have Spencer's weight press into him and force the stale carbon dioxide from his lungs.

On Spencer's exhale, Garrett inhaled, fresh and light. His head swam. Sparks flashed in his peripheral vision.

When the pain finally dissipated, Garrett opened his eyes to see Spencer's concerned expression and his lush lips, mere centimetres away, say, "I didn't mean '*no*, we can't do this'. I meant, '*no*, we *can* do this. I *want* to do this. But we can't in public. Not yet.' Because..."

"You're not out."

It wasn't something they could easily get around, but one thing was clear in Garrett's mind—whether it was worth the risk or not, he'd break the rules with Spencer any day. He wasn't going to give his whole heart. If he did that, and then Spencer ran, Garrett didn't think he'd be able to bounce back. But he could handle temporary. He could handle real.

"Are you sure?" Garrett didn't really want to give the man an out, but he needed to be sure Spencer wouldn't change his mind the minute they were no longer cocooned in the safe and secure bubble of Spencer's bed.

"I'm sure."

It was an answer, and...not.

Garrett waited for more, but nothing was forthcoming.

"So, to be clear," Garrett probed further. "We want to continue hanging out like this?"

"Yes."

"In private?"

"Yes."

"Till the week is over and I fly home?"

"Oh. Ah...yes"

"Okay then." He could handle that. "We just have to keep it quiet."

"Mm-hmm. Especially around the other players," Spencer concurred.

"And staff." Jesus, what would Toby say if he found out Garrett was fooling around with a player?

"And the media." Spencer added.

"For fuck's sake, Spencer. That's probably ninety percent of the people we cross paths with on a daily basis. At this rate, your apartment is the only safe place we'll be able to be together. Are we idiots to even think it's possible to hide a relationship?"

Spencer bit his lip. "Relationship?"

Shit! "Um." *Back pedal. Back pedal.* Garrett cleared his throat. "For lack of a better word."

Spencer stared at him for a long beat with those soft, moss-green eyes. Then he leaned forward, planted a kiss right over Garrett's heart, and said, "I'm good with that."

CHAPTER SEVENTEEN

Garrett

"Spencer!" A deep voice hollered from elsewhere in the apartment. "Wake up!"

"Kaz!" Spencer jerked up.

"Kaz? Who's that?" Garrett asked.

Neither of them had time to do anything, let alone cover themselves, before an older man appeared in the doorway.

When he saw them together in bed, he reared back. Garrett wasn't entirely sure, but it looked like the same guy who'd been with Lachlan in Spencer's playing box.

"Spencer!" Kaz yelled, sharp with anger.

"What the hell! What are you doing here?"

"What am *I* doing here? What are *you* still doing here? You were supposed to be on court half an hour ago."

"What? No!" Spencer flipped and reached for his phone beside the bed.

"You had a practice session with Callum this morning. I ran into him. You're lucky it wasn't his brother I ran into."

That stopped Spencer. "Shit. My match is tonight."

"Exactly. Where are your priorities?"

"Hey!" It didn't sit right with Garrett to hear Spencer being berated.

Spencer's hand came back to briefly touch Garrett's bare leg before slipping away.

Spencer stood up, leaving Garrett scrambling to cover himself with the comforter.

"Who's he? Some guy you—" the man's rant came to a screeching halt. "Oh, my God! You're that guy. That linesman." He pointed accusingly at Garrett.

"Line umpire," Garrett corrected.

"Leave him alone, Kaz." Spencer said. "Come on. Out." Spencer herded his coach out the door and down the hallway.

Left alone, Garrett could only arrive at one conclusion. "Well, this situation is officially fucked."

It felt wrong to let Spencer go off on his own to do battle with his coach. They'd gotten into hot water together. It made sense to get out of hot water together too. So, he tossed on his cum-scabby jeans, and padded down the shadowy hallway, close enough to hear Spencer's muttered protest.

"For fuck's sake, Kaz, I'm allowed to have a private life."

At the kitchen entrance, Garrett stopped. If either of them looked sideways, they'd see him, but he stayed quiet, not sure if he ought to make his presence known or not.

"Yes. But not at the expense of your career. And what's your plan here? He's an official. You're a player. Are you going to hide him and hope nobody notices? The man is pure kryptonite."

"He's just a crush!" Spencer cried out.

Garrett jerked himself back into the shadows.

Crush.

That single word dropped like lead in his gut.

Was that all he was to Spencer?

A crush?

Talk about kryptonite.

Bare minutes ago, he'd held Spencer's hand to his heart.

And it had felt so honest.

Earnest.

Real.

Nothing like a teenage fantasy.

Crush.

No wonder Spencer resisted being seen together in public. Garrett got the message loud and clear—*you don't break down a closet door for a crush...especially when you exist in the public eye*.

No matter how real their connection had felt, he shouldn't make any more of it than that one, little, word, because nobody stuck around for a connection as insignificant as a crush.

"You can't trust him," came Kaz's voice, clear as day.

"What are you talking about? You don't even know him."

"If he was trustworthy, he wouldn't be here, with you, breaking the rules."

"Every rule he broke, I've broken, too. And they're only rules, not laws. It's not like they're chiselled on stone," Spencer said.

"What if he outs you? We've been so careful to keep your sexuality private. Me. Your family. Everyone in your camp. We've all been so careful."

"He won't."

"But what if he does?"

"He won't." Spencer's voice rose. Insistent.

Garrett took a step out into the kitchen. "He's right."

They whipped around to face him.

"Who's right?" Kaz blurted the question. Distrust in his eyes.

"I won't out him."

"Says you."

"Says me." Garrett nodded. "Look. We met by accident, and broke the rules before we even knew there was a rule to break." His defence was weak. He knew it. But it was the only one they had.

Spencer nodded. "It happened, and now we're here."

Exactly. The facts were cut and dried. "Rules can't be unbroken."

Kaz did not look convinced. "When you're both done justifying your lies—" he started, but Garrett had to interrupt, because Spencer's coach was ignoring one very important component of their situation.

"Ever heard of MAD—mutually assured destruction?"

Kaz's eyebrows went up. "My father's name was Kazimov. What do you think?" he asked in a withering tone.

"Right. Then you know what it means to be dependent on each other's silence. Since I don't want to be exposed any more than he does, it's not in my interest to tell anybody anything."

"You're a distraction."

"Maybe so, but that doesn't mean I'll stop him from playing, or winning, or whatever the hell you think I'll do. I've seen him play. His talent is off the charts. He'll be a success no matter what you, or I, do. This," Garrett waggled a finger between him and Spencer, "is nothing. You heard him, I'm nothing more than a crush—a blip on his radar. But, if you don't have faith in your player, then..." Garrett left that cheap shot hanging.

Spencer gaped, wide-eyed, while his coach fumed.

"I have every faith in Spencer," Kaz gritted out.

"Then you've got nothing to worry about."

Kaz shut his mouth with a snap, and they should have left the confrontation there, but then Spencer had to ask, "What's the worst that could happen?"

Which, of course, lit another fire under his coach's arse.

"What the fuck do you mean *the worst that could happen*?" Kaz pointed his finger directly at Garrett. "He could lose his registration to umpire. And you," Kaz jabbed a finger at Spencer, "could be sanctioned by Tennis Australia, be thrown out of this tournament, and lose any hope of a wildcard to the Australian Open."

"Alright! Alright! You've made your point, Kaz. Thank you." Spencer looked mulish. Can you please, just, give us some space?"

"You want me to leave? Now?"

"Please."

"But—"

"I'll come find you in a bit. An hour, tops." Spencer crossed the lounge room to his front door and pulled it open. "Please."

The second the door was shut behind Spencer's irate coach, Garrett unwound his crossed arms and gripped the cold granite edge of the kitchen island behind him. "Fuck!"

"Yeah." Spencer had a pinched look about him. His shoulders tense. Like he was gearing up for a fight.

Garrett let go of the solid stone, willing himself to relax. "And here I thought bouldering would be the riskiest thing I'd ever do with you."

It took a minute to appear, but a wry smile eventually curled Spencer's lip. "We didn't actually go bouldering, Garrett."

Garrett waited for Spencer's eyes to meet his own before he said, "Oh yes, we did."

CHAPTER EIGHTEEN

Spencer

A blip.

Garrett's words cut.

Spencer's mind went back to their morning together.

They'd connected. For real. He knew it.

But...*a blip?*

It didn't feel like a blip in his heart.

They barely knew one another, but their connection had felt rock solid. Hell, he'd even said yes to a relationship. *A secret relationship*, he modified in his mind.

Perhaps Garrett hadn't really meant it. He could have just been trying to appease Kaz' concerns. Defending Spencer's honour, or some such gentlemanly move.

"Alright, so here's what we're going to do." Garrett glanced at the kitchen clock and winced. "I have to get to work. You make peace with your coach. We both go about our day. Do not say anything to anyone. Don't not let this...whatever this is...affect your match tonight. Then, after we've both had a chance to decide if we want this to continue, we reconvene and discuss a plan going forward."

Spencer thought they'd already decided to spend the week together, but if Garrett needed to regroup, he'd give him the time. A relationship, secret or otherwise, was not a one-way street. "Sounds like do not pass go. Do not pick up two hundred dollars."

"Yeah. But this isn't a game. This is your career."

"*Our* careers," Spencer asserted.

"No, Spencer. I've already lost my dream career. Yours is still standing."

Still standing? That image was too static for Spencer's liking. Win or lose, every match was a leap forward for his career. But at what cost?

The more time he spent with Garrett, the more he realised how narrow his world had become. There was so much more to life...and to him.

When was the last time he'd done anything with anyone, aside from Garrett, that didn't involve tennis? For all his talk about being valued by his Tennyson Bend mates for more than just his skill on court, when was the last time he'd done something completely non-tennis-related with them? Hell, even on Christmas day, they'd knocked a few balls around.

It got him thinking.

"Ever since I hurt my shoulder, I've held back. Mostly, it's been valuable. I've learned so much. Especially about myself."

"Patience," Garrett repeated Spencer's word from earlier.

"Yeah. But what if I took that too far?" Spencer recalled Garrett's other words—*his talent is off the charts*—he hated that word, but he took the intended compliment and let it burrow deep under his skin. "When we're together, I feel fully alive and present. When I play, though…" God, what was he trying to say? Had Spencer become so protective of himself, pushed back against his family's expectations, and exercised so much restraint that he'd actually stopped himself from playing his best?

"I always thought I was bringing every bit of me to the court. But I wasn't. Not everything. Not really. Not if I'm being honest." His time with Garrett had shown him that he could grow as both a man, and as a player. Which felt significant—so much more than a blip—and he couldn't let Garrett go without trying to explain the new well of energy and possibility he felt surging within.

"Everything…such as?"

"Such as letting my whole body feel the game. Such as…" he searched for a solid example, "Such as truly hearing the sound of the ball coming off the racquet. Not in a clinical, analytical way. More in a gut feeling, intuitive way."

"That's just the senses. We've all got those."

"Yes. It's base. And it's instinctual. It's all the extraordinary things I've felt alive to when we're together. So damn responsive." Spencer moved closer. "All I know is you, and I do become a caveman."

Garrett shifted on his feet. "And what's that got to do with tennis?"

"I thought my gift was focus—sustained concentration, taking each point, one at a time. But that effort is all in my head. Not in my body."

"And you realise now that you need to be more in your body? You got all that from a frott and a fuck?" Garrett clearly struggled to understand.

Spencer stepped toe-to-toe close, crowded Garrett up against the kitchen island, and gently slid the pad of his thumb up the silky skin of Garrett's inner arm.

A shiver ran through them both.

"See? Did you feel that? When we touch, my hair stands on end."

"It's hardly a surprise that we'd react physically to each other."

"Exactly. It's instinct. It's all the things I've rarely let myself have."

"Because you're still in the closet?"

"In part. Yeah." Could he tell Garrett that most men didn't turn him on even half as much as he had? That he'd never once before wrestled with the idea of coming out in order to be freely affectionate with a man? *Wait till you're sure of him, Spencer. Wait till you're sure that he's worth the risk.* "The point is that if I've suppressed those physical instincts by staying firmly in the closet, then how do I know I'm not suppressing other instincts elsewhere?"

"On court." Garrett nodded.

He gets it.

Spencer gave Garrett's elbow a quick squeeze, then dropped his hand, intending to step away. But Garrett didn't let him.

Garrett slung his arms around Spencer's waist in such a delicious boyfriend move that Spencer couldn't resist swaying forward, just a little bit.

"You're not actually saying sex and tennis are synonymous, are you?" Garrett asked.

"Ha! No. Can you imagine?"

"I *can* imagine—all those balls flying around—but I don't think tennis porn is really a thing."

Spencer shuddered. "Please don't ever use those two words in the same breath again."

Garrett flashed a smile, then his expression returned to thoughtful. "Are you saying that closing yourself off from your sexuality—from such a massive facet of who you are—could have had a dampening effect on your player's instincts?"

"Like a fire being quenched."

"And you need that fire on court?"

"Exactly." Spencer dropped his gaze and realised that at some point he'd placed his hand flat in the middle of Garrett's chest. Like it had a mind of its own, seeking home. "I leave a core part of myself in the locker room every time I step into the arena."

"So, what? You think fooling around ought to be part of your training now?"

Spencer snorted at the thought. "Yeah, right. Imagine what Kaz would think of that."

Garrett pursed his lips. "Seems everyone agrees that us fooling around is a bad idea."

"A very bad idea."

"But we're going to do it anyway." Not a question. A statement.

"Yeah." Spencer agreed, because he couldn't not agree.

Garrett looked away, then back again. Like he was strategiz-ing. "It's only truly a conflict of interest if we're on the same court at the same time."

The rationale wasn't strictly by the rules, but, in practice, Garrett wasn't wrong. "I guess."

"Work comes first. We stay professional," Garrett said with certainty.

Spencer wondered if Garrett realised how sexy it was when he took charge. "Definitely. I would expect nothing less."

"We just need to not screw up."

Spencer lifted his other hand and moved both to lightly rest over Garrett's shoulders. "Yes, to screwing. No, to screwing up."

Garrett ignored his cheesy joke and went on. "No more PDA. Even if we're sure we're alone in the wilds of nature."

"No PDA," Spencer parroted.

"No more excursions."

Damn. "But you just promised me the wilds of nature."

"Spencer." Garrett drew his name out.

"Okay. Fine. No more excursions to public places. Is that all?"

Garrett's nostrils flared. "It's you I'm trying to protect."

"I know, I know. It's just…" It was just that he wanted PDA. He wanted to be more than a blip on Garrett's radar. He wanted to be a goddamn *boom!*

"Eye on the prize, Spencer. If we're going to do this, we have to toe the line. The risk is too great."

Spencer nodded. "I know. And we will. I promise." He traced an x over his heart, then threaded his arms all the way around Garrett's neck and pulled him in. "Everywhere but here."

CHAPTER NINETEEN

Garrett

Toby raced up to him the minute Garrett swiped through the staff security entrance. "Hey, I didn't see you at breakfast this morning," he said.

"Oh, yeah. I was, ahh…" There must have been a million excuses he could have for leaving Toby's house at dawn, but Garrett's mind went blank. Garrett was very glad he'd taken the long route from Spencer's apartment building, around the outside of the tennis centre, rather than the more direct route through the tunnel. He had no idea what excuse he could have come up for having access to Tennyson Bend.

"Doesn't matter." Toby waved it off. "I'm glad I caught you before the meeting. Change of plan."

"What change?" Garrett's mind raced with the possibilities. "When?" *Please don't tell me I'm umpiring for Spencer's match tonight.*

"Ruth rejigged things and gamma crew will be on the outer courts today. Junior tournament. With the crew spread over two courts, you'll have to cover more lines. Think you're up to it?"

Oh, thank God. Not Spencer's match. The wave of relief set him tripping over his own words. "Yeah. Yep. Yes. I can do that."

"Are you sure? It's much more physically demanding. I can ask her to swap you to another crew for the day."

"No. It's fine. It's good. Really. No worries. Truly."

Jesus, Fellows. Get a grip.

Toby's eyebrows went up at Garrett's uncharacteristic verbal diarrhoea. "Ooo-kay. Great. Best get going, then." He led the way to the officials' antechamber where Ruth was giving out revised assignments to the grumbling crews. Few seemed pleased with the changes, but, so long as he wasn't expected to umpire on Spencer's court, Garrett didn't care. He grabbed his hat and a few bottles of water and made his way out with his crew to the outer courts allocated to the junior tournament with his crew.

They passed the two covered show courts, with a dozen rows of open stadium seating covered with a wide shade to protect the players, officials, and fans from the UV punch of the blazing Queensland sun.

Beyond those, the heat hit the hard blue courts without mercy. Grass courts would be cooler to play on, but they weren't practical in a sub-tropical climate prone to monsoon rains and extended droughts.

Outside the stadium, the complex was organized in two parallel rows of tennis courts with a wide path between, where tournament ticket holders could mill to watch their favourite players practice.

The courts to Garrett's right, sandwiched between the road and the visitors' path, were allocated to low-profile players. The first two courts on his left, between the visitor's path and a fallow green space, were allocated to the event's concurrent junior tournament. Beyond those, the courts were reserved for high-profile players to practice, since they drew a paying crowd everywhere they went.

His gamma crew wove through the gathering crowd and took up position on the junior tournament courts on the left.

To the teenage players, every match was do or die. To the tournament organisers, though, their matches didn't rank quite so high. So, instead of a full complement of line umpires, a crew like Garrett's was typically split over two or three courts. Which meant Garrett had to cover his line on both ends of the court.

Initially, he was glad to have reason to tighten his focus and shut out the rest of the world. The exponentially higher attention required was his comfort zone. In theory, with the conflict of interest between him and Spencer rendered moot by gamma crew's allocation, his conscience could take the day off. And it was working, until mid-way through a match between two highly strung fifteen-year-old girls. Between games, Garrett switched position from the baseline at the fallow end of the court to the ad court sideline at the visitor's end of the court.

While the girls were getting themselves sorted with the change of end, he backed up close to the chain-link fence in line with the service T and repeatedly squeezed the chain-links hard, forcing the wire diamonds out of their usual pattern then releasing them to return to their comfort zones. When play was about to start, he broadened his stance with his hands on his knees to stabilize his body and help focus his vision, then shifted of his weight onto his left leg, ready to race to the ad court sideline once the point was underway.

Just as the server tossed the ball high in the air and swung through, someone behind him yelled, "Yo, Bloom! You twat!"

Garrett jerked up and his arms flung wide.

It was an involuntary move, but that didn't matter—the damage was done.

Already off-balance, Garrett twisted awkwardly and a shard of nerve pain shot from his right hip to his toes. "Ah!" He cried out as he hobble-ran to cover the ad court sideline. The girl receiving backhanded the serve back into the far deuce court—an easy winner, but only because the kid serving didn't realise the ball was still in play.

Technically, Garrett hadn't called a fault, thank God, but his audible, and his involuntary action, were enough to confuse everyone on court. He straightened and shoved his knuckles hard into the space beside his spine, just above his right hip. It dulled the pain, but only slightly.

The receiver pumped her fist with victory. The server stayed in the same service position and geared up for a second serve. And, the chair umpire called, "Love-fifteen. Miss Kourin."

"What?!" the girl serving yelled, outraged, and pointed her racquet at Garrett. "He called a fault!"

"Shit," Garrett cursed under his breath.

It was tempting to stay quiet. It really was.

Even more than he wanted to stay quiet, he wanted to turn away from his court to look through the fence behind him to find the fucker who'd hollered Spencer's surname.

And—he didn't even bother to lie to himself about it—he wanted to see if his Spencer was nearby.

His Spencer.

Jesus, Fellows! Focus. Do your job. Speak. Speak up! Now.

He raised his left hand to the player in silent apology, and abandoned the fence to approach the chair umpire.

Unlike the first walk of shame he'd done that day, that one felt like a kick in the nuts.

Garrett prided himself on his accuracy. A ball was either in, or out. A play was by the book, or not. He was always on point. Reliably objective. It was the cornerstone of his reputation as a referee. But one mention of Spencer's name in range had him break from all of that.

He could feel the receiver's presence behind him, and the offended server closed in on the umpire's chair too—a mulish look on her face—gearing up for a fight.

Garrett's mind raced.

Umpires are human, he told himself. They made mistakes. But what possible reason could he give for that one?

I got distracted by someone calling out the name of the guy I shagged this morning.

God, no. That truth wasn't seeing the light of day.

He tried another tack.

A bee buzzed by my ear...caught me by surprise.

His gut protested. It just wasn't in him to lie—not outright. Which left him with a simple half-truth.

Garrett made eye contact with the chair umpire. "Someone behind me yelled out, and I involuntarily flinched." He turned to the player. "I apologise. Your serve was in."

"Yes!" she crowed, then looked to the umpire for an official correction.

"Are you sure?" The umpire scanned through the high fence. Probably looking for an obvious troublemaker.

If only he had eyes on the back of his head. But he dared not look around.

Not yet.

"Yes." He nodded. Of at least that he could be certain.

Her voice lowered. "And are you alright? Are you able to continue?" Her concerned gaze skimmed down his right side, but he wasn't about to use his dodgy leg as an excuse. Fuck, no.

He could sit, he could stand, and he could move. His injuries weren't the problem.

The problems were his out-of-control libido and a man by the name of Spencer Bloom.

"I'm fine." Or, he would be, as soon as he could successfully compartmentalize and banish Spencer to the 'no go' quadrant of his mind.

Failing that, he'd have to rely on every professional bone in his body.

She nodded at each of them, made a few notations on her tablet, then announced. "Correction, the serve was in. Replay the point. Two games to three. First serve, Miss Kourin."

If looks could kill, the receiver would have caused his fiery death, and Garrett knew he had some work to do to regain both players' trust.

That alone ought to have kept his attention on his toes as he returned to his position in line with the service T, but as soon he reached the back of the court his eyes rebelliously glanced up. Through two chain-link fences, and over dozens of people swarmed between, he saw a messy blonde man-bun, bobbing above the crowd.

Spencer.

"Shit."

So much for Kaz's worry about him distracting Spencer—what about Spencer's power to distract him?

The irony of that wasn't lost on Garrett as he again backed up to the chain-link fence, gave the diamonds one hard squeeze, then stared with deadly intensity down the line.

CHAPTER TWENTY

Spencer

Spencer shut the chain-link gate on the public spectators and lugged his tennis bag over to the net post where Kaz stood.

"Hey," he said. "All good?"

Kaz's shoulders tightened and he side-eyed Spencer for a second, then returned his focus to watching his doubles team run volley drills. "Make it punchier, Mitchell. You'll get walked over this afternoon if you don't get aggressive."

Guess Kaz isn't over it yet.

It went against the grain for Spencer to be at odds with anyone, and he was tempted to play up the grovelling just to smooth things over with his coach, but he was still smarting after the roast he'd received that morning.

Kaz was his tennis coach. Not his life coach. And, yeah, Spencer got that his psychological state mattered. Tennis was as much a mental game as a physical one. But he'd battled far more emotional hurdles in his career than the one Garrett presented. The secret they shared might be a burden, and being seen together might be a risk, but after his morning with Garrett, he felt more refreshed and grounded and alive than he'd felt in a long time.

What he and Garrett had done might have broken the rules, but something instinctive in Spencer drove him to protect it, despite the risk.

So, no, he wouldn't grovel.

He'd apologise to Callum for not showing up.

But he wouldn't apologise for something that felt so right. So necessary.

Even if they did have to keep it behind closed doors.

"Want me to help them warm up?" Spencer didn't wait for an answer, just squatted, unzipped his bag, and rifled through his gear for a practice racquet.

"Yo! Spencer!" Mitch twirled his racquet. "Come to show us your brilliance, have you?"

"Ha! Sure, Mitch. Y'got me. That's exactly why I'm here."

Mitch grinned. "Awesome. Take my side. Feed us some easy lobs." He scissor-kicked over the net to join his doubles partner.

Thomas rolled his eyes. "Guess it's lob-o'clock, then." He scooted a few steps back toward the service line and made a bring it gesture. "Show us what you've got, Bloom."

Feeding high balls and fielding stick wasn't exactly how he thought his morning practice session would go, but Spencer wasn't complaining. The last thing he needed was to get wound up and expend all his energy through the middle of the day. Eventually, he'd need to focus on his own game and opponent, but Mitch and Thomas came first. He could prep for his own match while they were out there doing battle.

Kaz gave the guys an occasional note, but for the most part he left them to it.

Must be nice to have that level of trust, he thought.

Missing the morning practice wasn't the worst thing out. But, as much as it annoyed him to admit it, Kaz might've been right that his little jaunt to Toohey Forest put his match preparation out of whack. For a night game, he'd usually have a solid morning practice hit, refuel, take a long rest, then discuss his game plan with Kaz before his usual pre-game warm up.

Between hits, Spencer bounced on the spot in an effort to shake off the nerves. His morning *had* been physical. Garrett had warmed him up, for sure. But that was different to being ready.

"Alright, guys, switch it up." Kaz directed. "Spencer, you up for some serves?"

"Sure." He looked Kaz's way. Since the man was finally talking to him, he guessed he'd earned his way out of the dog house. "Any particular serve they need to practice returning?"

"Nah. Mix it up. Keep them on their toes."

"No problem." He shuffled backward with the wheely ball basket to the baseline while Mitch and Thomas collected the fuzzy yellow strays and sent them back his way.

Once they'd finished using him for target practice, he pocketed a few balls and held up a fourth. "Who's first?"

"Bring it on, Bloom." Thomas took up position in the deuce court.

Spencer bounced the ball, then tossed it high.

"Foot fault!" Mitch yelled.

Spencer stumbled forward as he swung, missing the ball entirely. Thomas was already stretched wide for a phantom serve. While Mitch just stood there, cackling.

"Funny." Spencer grumbled.

"Boys! Get your act together."

Kaz's holler didn't do much to quell Mitch, but Spencer figured he probably wasn't in any sort of a position to push his luck with his coach.

He centred himself, toed the line again, and began his service motion.

Just as the ball reached its zenith, someone behind him called out, "Yo, Bloom! You twat!"

"Shit!" His racquet connected with the ball that time, but it caught the frame and took off like a rocket into the deep blue summer sky.

He spun around.

There, behind the chain-link fence, among a scattering of strangers who all seemed to be pointing smart phones his way, was Jerome Hargraves and his brother Callum.

Double shit.

"Well done, mate." Jerome sneered.

Callum smacked him across the chest with the back of his hand. "Be nice."

"Why?" Jerome looked puzzled. "He wasn't nice to you."

Callum sighed, all too used to his over-protective prick of a brother.

The British pair may have been related by blood, and they were equally wicked talented with racquet and ball, but that was about all they shared. Flip a coin between them and it was a fifty-fifty chance he'd get nasty or nice. As far as Spencer could tell, about Jerome's only positive quality was his unfailing support for his younger brother.

Spencer would spend time with Callum any day, and if he'd had his act together that morning, he would've been able to do just that. He could only blame himself for putting himself in the firing-line for Jerome's shit-stirring.

The two had been a fixture on the tour for years, drawing a devoted crowd, so Spencer figured it was probably wise to stay safe behind the chain-link fence and play nice, rather than return Jerome's snarly abuse.

Best not do that, Bloom.

Besides, Callum didn't deserve to have to deal with that crossfire.

"Sorry, mate." Spencer eyed Callum. "I was just..." *what can I say that isn't a lie?* "On another planet." *Planet Garrett.* "It probably won't help to know, but you're not the only person who I let down this morning." *Or the only person who expected something of me that I failed to give.*

"It's okay," Callum said in his toffee-soft Oxbridge accent. He didn't look at all put out, but Spencer knew he'd done a shitty thing.

"Won't happen again. I promise."

"You bet it won't." Jerome stuck his nose in. His accent was exactly the same as his brother's, but there was nothing soft about his snooty tone.

"Don't worry about it, Spencer. Seriously. I, ah...found someone else to practice with."

Jerome's eyes narrowed. "Yeah, that prick—"

"Give it a rest, Jerome." Pink streaked across Callum's cheeks. "Levi's not a prick."

Was the man blushing?

"Problem, fellas?"

Spencer whipped around. His heart racing. "Shit, Kaz. Don't sneak up on me like that."

But Kaz' attention wasn't on him. "Scoping out the opposition?" he asked the brothers.

"Opposition?" Spencer was confused. He didn't play doubles, and Callum was on the opposite half of the singles draw. Which meant the chance they were likely to compete against each other was about zero-point-zero-one percent. Unless some extreme, alternate-reality miracle came to pass, and they both made it to the final. Then he twigged. Was Kaz's team competing against the Brit brothers? "Are you guys up against Mitch and Thomas?" Spencer pointed a finger over his shoulder.

"This afternoon," Callum affirmed.

Jerome's eyes tightened into slits. "We don't need to spy to win."

"Then you boys won't mind moving on. Come on, Spencer." Kaz cupped the back of Spencer's neck with his solid hand. "Let's leave them to their preparation."

Kaz's fatherly touch was so familiar. It ought to have felt right—as though his coach had taken him back under his protective wing and restored their natural order.

So, why did Kaz's hand feel heavy?

Why did Spencer feel an inexplicable need to shrug it off?

Whatever the cause, Spencer couldn't shake off the feeling that it was time to stand tall on his own.

He kept pace with Kaz as far as the baseline, then said, "I'll help the guys warm up, then head off. Will I see you later this afternoon after their match?" He hated that he had to ask. Spencer might owe the man his best effort on court, but Kaz was his coach. He was there to do a job. He owed Spencer his professional support and attention.

"Of course," Kaz said.

"Great. Good. Okay." For all of Kaz's bitching and moaning about Spencer's choices off court, Kaz still seemed to be dedicated to their collective cause. That was good.

Spencer breathed out a sigh of relief, and grabbed a fresh ball from the basket.

"Who's next?"

His practice with Mitch and Thomas wasn't the ideal preparation for a simi-final singles match at a major tennis tournament. Doubles player positions and the larger court size meant he couldn't practice his shots or tactics the way he normally would before a big match. But Spencer made do. Any time striking the ball was helpful, and he'd long ago learned to adapt to changing circumstances.

A couple of hours later, he ducked back home to shower, refuel, and rest.

He'd just sat down at his kitchen bench and taken a mouthful of his usual pre-game meal, when *We are the Champions* jangled on his phone.

It was early for his mother's pre-match call, and he spared half a second wondering if he ought to be suspicious before he swiped the screen to answer, "'Lo, Mum."

"Darling. I just called to check in and wish you well for tonight." She sounded unusually perky. Which was saying something.

He chewed and swallowed. "Thanks."

"How are you feeling?"

"Okay." Spencer flicked the phone to speaker as he put it down on the kitchen bench and her voice filled the room.

"Just okay? Kaz said—"

"You talked to Kaz today?" he interrupted.

"Of course, darling. He is your coach."

"True." One day he'd point out that yes, Kaz was *his* coach. Not hers.

"He said you've been a bit distracted."

Spencer straightened. Had Kaz told her who he'd been spending time with? Did his mum know all the details? Or was she fishing for information?

"I thought we talked about this, Spencer. This is your chance. Your dream. You don't want to blow it on some..."

Damn! She knew everything.

"On some man?" he filled in her unsaid words.

There was an awkward pause. Then she raced on, "Oh, you know I don't care that you're gay. Birds of a feather, and all that. But, Spencer, if it gets out now, that'll be the story. The media won't notice how well you play. They won't recognise your achievements. They won't realise that you're a star."

"Low on the horizon," he pointed out the obvious.

"What?"

"If I'm a star, I'm hanging pretty damn low on the horizon."

...and not too bright.

There was a pause on the line.

"Let's get back to the point, Darling."

Oh, yes please, his inner teenager snarked, *let's get back to you telling me how to live my life.*

No, thank you.

"What are you all up to before the game?" He didn't need to ask if they'd be watching, but it was usually a safe topic to fill a minute or two of conversation.

As she answered, Spencer ate the last few bites of his meal, rinsed the plate, stacked it in the dishwasher, then rounded the kitchen bench to his wall calendar.

He picked up the marker and flipped it between his knuckles—over, under, over, under—while his mother spoke.

"...and the Kazimovs are joining us for an early dinner at the pub before we watch your match. Dozens will be there, darling, all cheering you on. All your fans. I can't wait to see you win."

"No pressure, then."

"I have faith in you, Spencer. You just have to envisage holding up that trophy, and you'll get the win."

"Right." Easy as that, huh? The blank square on his calendar reminded him of a kids tv program he used to watch when he was really young—before tennis—with different shaped windows to dream through.

Through that square window, he didn't see tennis, or trophies, or his family pressing him to win, win, win. He saw dawn light, and rough rocks, and Garrett's orgasm-wrecked face staring straight back at him.

Spencer uncapped the marker and wrote in the blank square:
BOULDERING WITH GARRETT

Then he recapped the marker, and stepped back.

My life. My choices. My success.

Like a dog pissing on his territory, it felt good...so good, to reclaim his life, one dream at a time.

Yes, he loved tennis.

Yes, he wanted to win.

But it wasn't everything.

Not by a long shot.

"Thanks for the call, Mum, but I've gotta go rest. Kaz's orders. Give my love to Dad and Bryce and Casey," Spencer gave his farewell and hung up.

...Twelve hours later, Spencer dropped his racquet and collapsed, spread-eagled, on the court.

He'd get up in a second to go shake Herc's hand.

For just a moment, though, Spencer let himself stop and feel the thunder of the crowd reverberate through his skin, and bask in the starry glow of a thousand camera flashes, shining bright for him.

CHAPTER TWENTY-ONE

Garrett

"Yes!" Garrett pumped the air. *He did it!*

"Fan, are we?" One of the guys from the off-court half of the beta crew asked, surprising Garrett. It wasn't like they were invisible, or particularly quiet, but he'd been so engrossed in the game, he'd forgotten they were even there. They sat around a table, playing cards, while the other half were upstairs on centre court, calling Spencer's match.

Jesus. He'd have to be more careful if he wasn't going to give the truth away.

"Leave him alone, Shane," a fifty-something woman at the table said. "If I wasn't on duty, I'd be glued to the tv, too. And, speaking of triumphant," she threw a quick wink Garrett's way then tossed down a card, "Ace."

The rest of them groaned and threw in their cards.

When Garrett turned back to the television screen, Spencer stretched to shake the chair umpire's hand, then flopped down on the player's bench, tilted his head back, and closed his eyes. His lips moved, like he was saying something, but Garrett

couldn't hear. He looked reverent. Almost like he was pray-
ing to the heavens.

"Mind if I switch the sound on?" he asked the group at
large as he stretched to turn up the volume. The network
had shifted focus away from Spencer to his opponent, Herc
Georgiou, but the commentators, still blathering in their
courtside bunker, weren't so easily diverted.

"...the last thing you'd expect of this young man."

"Not so young, Jack. He's twenty-four years old. Was in
and out of the tour a couple times due to a left shoulder
injury, if my memory serves correct."

"I didn't see any indication of shoulder trouble tonight,"
Jack said.

"Nope. And at six four, he's got the wingspan to get some
serious power behind those shots."

"Which he needed against Herc Georgiou tonight."

"Yep. Georgiou didn't lose this match. Bloom beat him.
Fair and square."

"I dare you to say that to Herc's face." Jack chuckled.
"What I'm most impressed by is Bloom's grit. Georgiou
tried everything to shake him, but Bloom kept his nerve. He
went out there believing he could win, and he did the job."

"Yes, he did. From here on out, I'll be paying close attention to Spencer Bloom."

"He's one to watch, that's for sure."

"And, I believe now we're going to hear from the man
himself."

The screen filled with vision of Aaron Stevenson, ex-pro, now commentator, as he followed a black-clad media tech with a stand-up microphone onto the court.

His no-longer-anonymous Achilles, looking adorably sheepish, stepped up to it and into the spotlight.

The crowd were on their feet.

This is where it begins, Garrett thought.

"Spencer Bloom," Aaron's voice boomed around the stadium.

"That's me."

The crowd's wild cheer left Spencer looking stunned.

When they finally quieted down, Aaron said, "Congratulations, Spencer, that was three brutal sets."

"Yeah. I gave just about everything. Lucky for me, tonight that was enough."

"Lucky for us, too. A lot of these good people watching here and on their televisions at home are discovering you for the first time this week. What's it like to be the new hometown hero?"

"Hero? Me? All I do is play tennis, mate. Heroes are people who make a real difference in the world."

Garrett couldn't help crack a laugh at that. He felt the presence of others behind him in the official's room, but didn't spare a look. All of his attention was on the screen.

"That's an admirable attitude," Aaron said.

Spencer shrugged, and Garrett could practically read his mind—*it's the truth*.

"Well, you proved yourself tonight. You were all over that court. Herc is a fierce competitor, and you certainly proved yourself against him."

Spencer nodded. "He's a tough opponent, but I've had the advantage of seeing him play many times."

"You had insight into his game?"

"Exactly."

"But you still had to step up—bring your A-game."

The microphone caught Spencer's breathy laugh. "More like my A-plus game, but, yeah, I'm happy with the way I moved around the court. Made a few good volleys at opportune moments. Kept the ball in play—which you have to do to have any hope against Herc. His passing shots are incredible."

"And you kept your cool."

Spencer gave an aww shucks grin that the crowd clearly loved. "No tantrums this time."

"No foot faults, either."

"Ha! No. Thanks for the reminder, Aaron. Appreciate it." His obvious sarcasm drew more chuckles.

"Talking about your serve? That was an impressive display. A cracking ninety-four percent of first serves in. One-hundred percent for the third set. That's nearly unheard of."

Spencer didn't look surprised. "Yeah, I was pretty happy with that."

"Humble, too. Bet the ladies like that."

Garrett stiffened. How would Spencer answer that?

Spencer shrugged and said nothing, but the wolf-whistles from the audience came thick and fast.

"So, what's your secret sauce?"

"Jeez, Aaron. Now I'm hungry." Spencer lifted his shirt a few inches to rub his stomach, producing another round of wolf-whistles and cat-calls, and Spencer ducked away from the microphone for a second. When he returned, his cheeks looked suspiciously pink. "No secret sauce. I just felt...good."

"Simple as that?"

Spencer quirked a smile. "Ever heard of the kiss principle?"

"I think we've all heard of kissing." From the noise in the stadium, the crowd agreed with Aaron. "Care to elaborate?"

"Kay, eye, ess, ess— kiss—keep it simple, stupid."

"Hmm...not a bad strategy. Though it looked far from simple from where I was sitting. What do we think, Brisbane? Want to see Spencer Bloom do more kissing on court?" He asked the crowd, and they gave a rousing cheer in response. "I think that means yes."

"Thanks, Aaron, you're the best." His droll tone dripped sarcasm, but his gaze diverted away from Aaron and landed directly on the close-up camera, where those moss-green eyes, usually clear as glass, had become the dark wells of a man battling overwhelm.

Fight or flight?

Through the screen, Spencer seemed to stare directly at Garrett.

It couldn't have lasted for more than half a second, but Garrett felt it deep.

He swayed forward, drawn by instinct.

Then Spencer looked away, the sound of the crowd rushed in, and the camera pulled back to show full-body shots of him and Aaron. And Garrett just about stumbled over his toes to stay close.

Aaron raised his microphone. "Talking about feeling the love, rumours are flying around that you've been granted a wildcard entry to the Australian Open. What do you think about that?"

Spencer pulled a shock-horror expression. "Shh! Don't jinx me!"

Aaron flashed his media-white grin. "Oops, sorry."

The interview continued, but Garrett didn't hear their words.

His mind was reeling.

He'd heard Kaz mention the Australian Open during his reprimand of Spencer that morning, but it hadn't really registered.

Spencer...at the AO...in Melbourne...in Garrett's home city...in his bed...where they could...

His brain came to a screeching halt.

What the hell am I thinking about me and Spencer in Melbourne? We have to survive the week in Brisbane first.

If he gave up officiating in tennis for good—and that was a very big *if*—then he could begin to consider what came next.

That was, if Spencer stuck around.

But, again, he was getting ahead of himself. A sensible man would pull back to protect himself.

He couldn't get too caught up in their wild attraction.

A blip—that was what Garrett had called their connection. He hadn't meant it. Not exactly. But he wasn't about to admit his true feelings out loud. He wasn't an idiot—masochistic or otherwise.

So, no. He'd not let himself be pulled in any deeper than he already was. He'd enjoy a satisfying fling for the remainder of the week, then get on with fixing the shit-show fate had made of his real life. Because the one thing he could be sure of was nobody was coming to rescue him from those ashes. It was up to him to decide what came next, and then to take action.

With that determined life plan sorted, Garrett tuned back into the on-court interview.

"In all honesty," Spencer said, "getting to compete at the Aussie Open would be a dream come true. I've been a bunch of times as a spectator. But to play there for real? Maybe even on Rod Laver Arena? That'd be surreal."

"And what about off court dreams?" Aaron asked. "Anyone special you'll share this win with? A girlfriend, perhaps?"

"Nah." Spencer ducked his head, abashed. It was ridiculously cute.

"You don't look too sure about that."

"Well…I do have a lucky charm. Sort of. Maybe." A blush stole across his cheekbones.

Lucky charm.

Could Spencer mean him?

A chilly tendril wormed down Garrett's spine.

He wasn't lucky. Not recently, anyway. Though things had been looking up since he met Spencer.

"I like the sound of that." Aaron grinned as though he knew something secret. Which of course he didn't, but Garrett tensed anyway. He firmed his spine and crossed his arms.

When Spencer didn't add any further comment, Aaron's grin faltered, but the media training eventually kicked in. "Love it. Let's hope she brings you luck in the semi-final. Put your hands together, everyone, for Spencer Bloom." Aaron encouraged the crowd and they went wild as Spencer turned to wave at each of the four sides of the stadium.

"Hey," came a voice over Garrett's shoulder.

He jerked around, wrenching at least twelve dozen muscles in the process, and probably a few bones too. "Shit, Toby!"

"Sorry. Didn't mean to sneak up on you. I'm heading home in a few." Toby shook his car key. "Want a lift?"

"Oh, ah." Garrett looked back around to the television, but a flashy commercial for some new tech gadget filled the screen.

Had Spencer already left the court? Where was he?

In his mind's eye, Garrett tracked Spencer's likely pathway through the building from court level to the locker room to the smaller rooms for trainers and physios where he'd trapped Garrett up against a massage table and claimed his—

"Garrett?"

"Huh?"

Toby was frowning with concern. "You alright, mate?"

"Yeah, yeah. Sure." *No, not really.* "I'm fine. Good." Toby didn't look entirely convinced, but Garrett didn't care. "Thanks for the offer, but I could do with the walk." He did a vague sort of stretch, rocked on his feet, and didn't even try to hide an obnoxious smirk. "It's not too far, and I'm a bit stiff after my bastard of a boss made me run around in the sun all day."

Toby's brow went up. "Bastard, eh?"

"That's the general consensus." Toby was so easy to tease...and distract. Thank God. Garrett did not want to explain why he'd stood rivetted to Spencer's match for so long that practically every tense muscle in his body had seized up.

Toby rolled his eyes. "You sure? Hamish messaged saying he has a bottle of Chardonnay chilling in the fridge with our names on it."

"Yep. I'm sure. Don't wait up for me."

By the time Toby was gone, the run of commercials had finished and the commentators began their match post-mortem, but Garrett didn't need to see re-plays. He needed to see the man in the flesh—present tense.

And future.

Most likely, Spencer would have retreated to the locker room for a shower, maybe debrief with Kaz. Garrett figured he had at least half an hour to kill, but he didn't have anywhere else to be, so he grabbed his knapsack and trailed out of the officials' antechamber to the long bright-lit corridor.

It was probably only his conscience that made Garrett feel conspicuous as he picked a spot a few metres down from the player's locker room entrance and leaned up against the cold concrete besa block wall. He tried to strike a pose that said 'innocuous' to the masses, but 'unmissable' to Spencer, then settled in to wait.

Lucky charm.

Just as Garrett fell into the daydream those remembered words inspired, the locker room door opened and Spencer stepped out.

He was looking down at first, thumbing his mobile phone, a tangle of sweaty hair curtained his face in shadow. Still wearing the t-shirt and shorts he'd sweated through on court, he carried a mussed towel over one shoulder and his hefty tennis bag over the other. He looked like he'd run a marathon.

The heavy fire door shut behind him with a thunk, prompting him to look up to the left, then to the right, and their eyes met.

"Lucky charm?" Shit, Garrett hadn't meant to ask that.

Ugh. Now I've made things awkward.

The tip of Spencer's tongue licked his upper lip, then disappeared, and he gave a subtle tilt of his head to the right, to where the corridor ended with the swipe-lock door through to Spencer's apartment building.

It was a clear come hither, and Garrett's held breath rushed out.

He leaned down, picked up his knapsack, and followed after his man.

CHAPTER TWENTY-TWO

Spencer

Spencer woke to the feeling of Garrett's fingers drifting around his rib cage and down the length of his spine.

He lay spread-eagled, face down, three-quarters on top of Garrett's hairy chest, with his left hand tucked beneath the pillow beside Garrett's head and their legs twined like two strands of DNA.

Spencer couldn't remember the last time he'd ever felt so warm or comfortable with another soul.

"How are you feeling? Not too sore?" Garrett's fingers tickled as they reached the dip just above Spencer's arse and drew a circle...or was it a 'G'?

Yes, please. Sign your name. Claim me.

GF + SB 4 Eva.

Under the pillow, where Garrett couldn't see, Spencer scribed with his finger a heart. As though Valentine's cupid had come six weeks early.

What they had wasn't love. They barely knew each other...but daydreams couldn't hurt. Could they?

The warm hand skimmed up again to cup his shoulder and squeeze.

That touch didn't feel intimate anymore. It felt more like a masseuse's touch. Impersonal. Like how a physio might rub him down after a game. And he realised Garrett wasn't asking if his arse was sore after their epic celebration sex. He was asking if the rest of him was sore after his quarter-final win.

"A bit," he admitted, honestly answering both questions in one, then slid sideways a few inches and tucked his face into the dark nook of Garrett's pit to hide his blush.

The man smelled so good.

Why did he smell so good?

All hazelnuts and vanilla. Sweet and savoury. Spencer wanted to lick him all over.

He pulled his left hand out from under the pillow and lay it flat over Garrett's heart. It wasn't tripping like his was. In fact, he couldn't feel a thing. Not a heartbeat. Not even a vague thrum. Nothing but the quiet rush of Garrett's steady breath.

Garrett stretched his legs and shifted his hips. Restless. "Aaron was right when he called your match brutal. Ever gone toe-to-toe like that for five sets?" He asked in a low, sleepy rumble.

Spencer groaned. "Nope. Don't wanna." Nor did he want to talk about Hercules Georgiou, or his next opponent, or any other future-fantasy tennis match. Reality would come soon enough, but he didn't want to invite it in to their bubble. Not yet.

Under the guise of a stretch, Spencer slid further up Garrett's body and reached to kiss the scratchy day-old growth beneath

Garrett's chin. An open-mouthed kiss designed to fire the man up. And his hand drifted south.

"What are you doing?" Garrett asked.

"Nothing."

"Hmm...doesn't feel like nothing."

"What does it feel like?"

"Like...something."

He gave Garrett's half-hard cock a stroke. "You're such a wordsmith."

"Hey, don't belittle the dude with the dick."

Spencer bit his lip. It felt like a laugh was welling up in his heart, which was all kinds of ridiculous. That organ was for pumping blood, for delivering oxygen to his body. Not for...whatever he was feeling.

"And such an awesome dick it is." He let go long enough to give it a little pat on the head. *Good boy.*

"Hmm..." Garrett drowsily shifted, his hips chasing Spencer's hand. "You looking for a repeat, are you?"

"The same?" The technicolour movie of what their night together ran in Spencer's mind—Garrett, in the shower, returning the favour. Just the thought of it set lightning off in his balls. But no, that wasn't what he had in mind.

He eased in closer to Garrett's side, dropped a teasing kiss into the hollow above his clavicle, then stretched to whisper into his ear, "Not exactly."

"Hmm. Then what did you have in mind...exactly?"

Garrett's carotid thrummed and the hollow Spencer had been loving deepened as Garrett raised his head to look south.

Spencer looked too.

Were they seeing the same sight? He wondered.

Garrett's roused nubs that peeked through the dark curls on his chest, the jerky rise and fall of his belly as his diaphragm quickened, the swollen head of his rouge-red cock held firm in Spencer's fist, and the sheeny pearl of pre-cum that welled silver in the dawn light.

They'd get to what he had in mind, but first Spencer had to taste.

He rocked his hard cock into Garrett's hip, planted a hot, open-mouthed kiss to Garrett's thrumming carotid and scooted south. Another night, he promised himself, he'd take his time, but Spencer had his eye on the prize.

He lifted up and over Garrett's body to land on his knees, straddling Garrett's thighs, perfectly situated to taste his salty essence. Making a show of it, Spencer gathered the pearl with his tongue, swirled around the head, then took him into his mouth and sucked, deep.

"Mmph!" Garrett squirmed with need, but Spencer grabbed for his hipbones and held him firmly in place. He wanted to give Garrett pleasure, not pain, and the last time Garrett had accidentally twisted his lumbar spine, the pain had left him white-face and shaking.

Fingernails scoured through Spencer's loose hair as he sucked Garrett down as far as he could take him. Not pushing. Garrett wasn't rude like that. And Spencer rewarded him with a hum that he knew would feel like heaven.

"Need you in me," Garrett moaned in answer.

But that wasn't what Spencer had in mind.

He pulled back a little, dragged his spit-slick lips up Garrett's thick shaft in an obscene manner, then set to lashing every inch with his tongue. It was enough stimulation to keep Garrett simmering, but not coming out of his skin—safe enough, Spencer hoped, to release his hips and multi-task.

He held the base of Garrett's shaft with one hand and ran the tip of his tongue down the underside, teasing both of them, while he reached across the bedding with the other to grab the lube and flip the lid. Fingers slicked, he raised his arse cheeks—a peacock on display—and reached back to massage his own hole.

"What?" Garrett asked, his breath thready. But Spencer didn't bother to explain his actions.

Pupils blown, cheeks flushed, lungs heaving, Garrett looked enthralled as he watched the tell-tale movements of Spencer's wrist, circling with the tip of his index finger until he felt the pulse of his greedy ring drawing him inside.

It didn't take long to stretch himself. He wanted to feel Garrett's full girth inside him almost as much as he wanted to feel Garrett around him...consuming him.

He gave Garrett's cock one last loving suck, earning him a run of incomprehensible curses, and a rough tug on his hair. He shmeared the slick from his finger onto the already-ruined bedsheet and reached for the last condom. Spencer could have asked for Garrett's assistance, but he was determined to take care of his man. He tore the packet open with his teeth and sheathed Garrett's impressive cock.

"Roll onto your side," he said, with an insistent hand to Garrett's hip.

"I'm not an invalid," Garrett protested, but he quickly got with the program when Spencer slotted himself into place as the little-spoon and hooked the top of his foot around Garrett's right knee—drawing him in tight. "Oh."

"Is that a good 'oh'?"

"That's a very good 'oh'," Garrett rumbled.

Spencer pushed out his arse in a slow undulation, loving the feeling of Garrett's thick cock riding his crack so much that he did it again, and again. The only thing that'd make it better would be to have Garrett inside him. "Fill me up," he insisted.

"Yeah?"

Spencer nipped at the soft skin on the inside of Garrett's left arm, then licked it better. "Slow and deep."

"Bossy bottom."

No. He just knew what he wanted, and was in the habit of going after it.

He went to reach between them, but Garrett swiped his hand away.

Garrett pulled back far enough to let a goose-bumping whisp of airconditioned air in before he lined up to Spencer's entrance, and pressed inside.

"Oh, my fucking God, that feels so good." A whole new ripple of goose bumps shimmied up Spencer's spine.

His muscular ring inside resisted the breach, but neither of them paid much mind to that.

Garrett's right arm came around him and his hand, spread wide, pressed firm across his belly, as though Garrett expected Spencer to disappear on him. No way in hell was that happening. He was right where he wanted to be.

But it was impossible to stay still. Not while every nerve ending fired white hot.

His toes curled as he rocked back, inch by inch, onto Garrett's cock. Hot breath coasted across his shoulders, chased by bites and licks and wet, sucking kisses. And neither of them bothered to curtail the shuddering groans that came when Garrett was finally seated, deep inside.

Spencer wove his fingers through Garrett's, placed a kiss on the lifeline bisecting Garrett's palm, then closed their collective fist and held it tight to his heart. "Perfection," he said. And it was.

Then, he began to move.

CHAPTER TWENTY-THREE

Spencer

Garrett log-rolled away from him, and groaned as he reached for his phone beside the bed. "We should get up."

Lines on his skin from the rumpled bedsheets warred with the long pink surgical scar that rippled down the lower half of Garrett's spine. Knobbly in places, smooth in others. It wasn't raw anymore, but it was obvious to Spencer that the hurt was fresh. Instinct told him to touch—to soothe—but he'd noticed Garrett was sensitive when it came to his injuries, so Spencer stayed his hand.

Instead, he stretched, feeling the delicious pull in every single muscle and tendon and ligament. "Don't wanna," he said through a yawn. God, how long since he'd had such a good sleep?

His back still to Spencer, Garrett swung his legs slowly off the side of the bed and sat up. "If you miss practice again, Kaz will kill you."

"Still don't wanna." He'd hang on as long as he could to the warm, fuzzy morning.

"And I have to get to the gym before work. I was so stiff last night—"

"Yeah, you were." Spencer flicked Garrett's hip playfully.

"Behave."

"Don't wanna." He didn't want to go anywhere.

"Is that your answer for everything? Don't wanna get up. Don't wanna go to practice. Don't wanna behave. Don't wanna—"

"Leave."

Garrett's shoulders squared, rigid. "But you will."

Unable to see the man's face, Spencer tried to read his body language, "You know, a part of me wishes I'd lost last night. If I wasn't playing anymore, we'd be free to do whatever the hell we like."

Garrett stood and crossed to the window. He pushed open the heavy curtains, letting a shaft of bright summer sunlight in. "You're too much of a competitor to wish for that."

"True," he had to concede, "but in different circumstances, I wish..." He padded his fingertips across the still-warm sheets where Garrett had slept.

Could he say what he really wished? Was it safe to admit his innermost thoughts?

"What do you wish?" prompted Garrett, after the silence between them had stretched out too long.

His gut told him Garrett was honourable. Dependable. He met the man's gaze, "I know it's nobody else's business but ours, but, still, I wish we didn't have to hide as though we're doing something wrong."

"We *are* doing something wrong."

"Ugh. That's not what I mean."

"You could come out. Plenty of openly queer tennis players have had success. You wouldn't be alone."

"Women, maybe. Not so much from the men's draw. I have no interest in being the lightning rod to that bag of bullshit."

"You did say you wanted to bring your authentic self to the game," Garrett annoyingly pointed out. "In or out, it's your decision."

"Ugh. Stop being so rational." Spencer covered his eyes with his forearm. "It's nobody else's business," he re-asserted.

Garrett turned to him at the window, his face thrown into shadow by the bright morning light behind him. "Are you afraid to win?"

"What?" Where had that come from? "No. What makes you ask that?"

"It's classic sports psychology. Winners have further to fall."

Stunned, Spencer couldn't think of a single thing to say, except, "God, Garrett. Cynical much."

Garrett shrugged. "You think you're only competing in tennis. That the crowd is only judging you by the score on the board. But if you put your true self out there, then the game shifts. It expands. Suddenly, they're not just judging your shots. They're judging who you are as a person. It's risky."

"Well, aren't you just a bright ray of sunshine, today."

"I'm trying to be realistic."

Spencer pulled himself upright and shifted to sit bolstered by the head of the bed. "I'm not afraid."

"Okay."

"I'm not," Spencer insisted. "I just don't think every ten-nis-loving Aussie has a right to know everything about my personal life. Even if I am a public figure."

"Even if you're a champion."

"Ha! Not likely. But, yeah. Even then."

"I've seen you play. You have it in you."

Spencer had to look away. Garrett knew tennis. He knew what it was to be a champion. He wasn't giving false plati-tudes. If Garrett thought Spencer could make it, maybe he really did have a chance.

Garrett leaned forward and lightly stroked a finger-tip across Spencer's forehead—temple to temple. "Even if you're wearing the crown of glory."

Spencer blinked. "Is that how you see me?"

Garrett answered with a lava-hot gaze that trailed down Spencer's naked body, and back up again. Then he leaned in deep for a long, lazy kiss.

With a last, gentle sweep of his tongue along Spencer's bottom lip, Garrett pulled away.

Spencer hummed.

God, I could stay in this safe, warm cocoon forever.

It was perfect.

Too perfect—like a storybook house, surrounded by a white picket fence.

Only their house, Spencer knew, was edged with wicked, thorny roses.

Eventually, the prick would come and their bubble would burst. But, not yet.

"What are you up to today?" Spencer asked. Since he wasn't playing, there was no way Garrett's court assignment would be a problem.

Garrett groaned. "God knows. Ruth likes to change up the court assignments at the last minute. Keep us on our toes. What about you?"

"I'm a fan of Plan A."

"What's that?"

"Misbehaving with you. Here. In bed."

"Mmm. Sounds good. And plan B?"

"Behaving."

Garrett snorted softly. "Sounds awful."

"I know, right." But if he had to behave, he would—a warm-up hit with Callum; a gentle workout in the gym; a massage with the local physio; a tactics session with his coach; good food; and rest—proving to Kaz that he didn't need his hand held to be professional.

Nobody had to know that the only time he managed to divert his mind from Garrett was during his hour-long afternoon nap. Or that he had to take it on his couch. Because, his over-eager dick would never let him get any rest if he lay down on his still mussed, cum-smeared sheets.

Opportunities to advance to an ATP final didn't come around too often. And after all that good behaviour, Spencer felt primed. Everything went to plan until he clashed with lanky Dutchman, Levi Bakker, and promptly lost the first set 0-6, barely getting a look in.

Crush wasn't too harsh a word to describe it.

Not the good kind of crush.

Nothing like the can-never-get-enough whenever Garrett Fellows was within reach type crush.

No. This was the bad kind of crush.

The kind he wanted to escape from down a deep dark hole.

Spencer couldn't help looking up to his player's box—seeking support—but the only person sitting there was Kaz, alone in the front row, surrounded by empty chairs, his fists clenched knuckle-white over the railing and his face carefully blank.

Spencer kicked himself for not inviting at least one of his friends to come to the match. Conflicting work commitments had kept Lachlan away, and he very much doubted Dane would have thought a tennis match important enough to leave his office. But he could have asked Brady to come along. For something so important to Spencer, his friend would surely have told his wonky biorhythms to fuck off so he could stay awake past noon. Or he could have invited some of his students. Surely, Amy deserved a place there.

Of course, the face Spencer really wanted to see up there was Garrett's.

Where was he?

Was he watching the game?

Was he disappointed in Spencer's performance?

Did he believe Spencer could turn the match around?

Did he still think Spencer deserved the mighty crown of glory?

At 0-1 in the second, having just lost his service game to love...again...Spencer collapsed in his seat at the changeover of ends and threw a towel over his head. It didn't render him invisible or keep out the disappointed murmurings from the audience, but he couldn't do much about that.

Buck up, Bloom. You're down. But you're not out. Not till the last point is lost.

It was a good pep talk.

Simple.

Direct.

But it didn't do him much good.

Chapter Twenty-Four

Garrett

From love-one down, second set, Garrett couldn't watch anymore. If he'd had a towel handy, he'd have thrown it over his own head, just as Spencer had on the changeover.

How could true fans of the sport bear to watch?

Team sports like footy were so different. The wins and losses were spread around so nobody could take too much credit or too much blame. But a solo sport like singles tennis? Shit. That was like falling on your own sword.

His tangle of emotions felt like a wire scourer—messy and harsh and far too real.

He knew he shouldn't be so invested. They'd agreed what they were up to was temporary, and Garrett had tried his best to keep deep feelings out of the mix, but there was nothing shallow about the agony he felt watching Spencer get railroaded by the number four seed.

It wasn't so much that Spencer was playing badly. He wasn't making bad plays, or masses of unforced errors. It was just that Levi Bakker was having a stellar night.

With another inch on Spencer's six foot four, Bakker had the wingspan of an albatross, and he used it to his advantage. The angles he achieved were masterpieces. Every single shot seemed to find the lines or corners, pushing Spencer so far out of court that all he could do was stretch and bunt the ball back...if he could reach it at all.

Levi was a freight train, and Spencer was tied to the tracks.

Garrett flicked off the television in the officials' antechamber and went to grab his gear from the staff locker.

"Heading out?" Cate asked.

He pulled from his knapsack the t-shirt and shorts he'd packed, anticipating he might need a change of clothes if Spencer welcomed him back into his apartment...and into his bed. But Cate didn't need to know that.

"Gym." He shut the locker door with a metal-on-metal clang that rang in his ears.

Jesus. He wasn't normally a nervous nelly, but Spencer's match had him rattled.

He pocketed his locker key and flashed a brief wave. "See you later."

"I'm off too. It's been nice to work with you, Garrett. Where are you off to after Brisbane? Did you get a spot umpiring for any of the other AO warm up tournaments? Sydney? Or Adelaide?" She seemed intent on starting a conversation, but that wasn't the distraction he needed. He'd enjoyed working with the woman, but Garrett didn't want to get caught up—he had places to be, things to do, tennis to ignore.

"Nah."

If his colleagues wanted to know who he was and where he was from, there was more than enough information out there on the internet to get a solid picture. If they wanted to know where he was going next...well, get in line. It was hard enough coping with life one day at a time, let alone figuring out what his far horizon might look like.

A vision of Spencer's gorgeous face flashed in his mind, and Garrett's breath hitched at the thought of a future with him. But that wasn't on the cards, and he shrugged the possibility away as he retreated to the relative safety of the gym. A half hour on the treadmill ought to exhaust the tension that wracked his body and get his mind off the match above. Win-win, he thought.

Garrett powered up the machine and raised the incline—no way did he want a repeat of his last embarrassing treadmill incident.

He was just congratulating himself on a job well done for staying vertical when he looked up and noticed the mirrors that ran the full length of the wall in front of the cardio machines. It was impossible to not look into them—unless Garrett closed his eyes and prayed that he didn't fall flat on his face. Again. And, of course, reflected in those mirrors were a bank of three television screens, all tuned to the live feed of Spencer's and Levi's match unfolding on centre court.

"Ugh. For fuck's sake!" Could he not catch a break?

Then he noticed the score.

5-5

"Fuck!"

What a turnaround!

Spencer was killing it in the second set.

Garrett pressed the big red emergency stop button on his treadmill and the whole thing came to a shuddering, still tilted, halt. He grabbed for the 'oh shit' bar to save himself, but ninety-nine percent of his attention was on the mirror and Spencer's frazzled-looking visage.

Sweat dripped from Spencer's nose. His man bun hung askew. His pale shirt had turned slate grey. And every visible inch of skin sheened with sweat.

Steadied, Garrett turned to face the gym. Then he realised his mistake.

Not 5-5...

2-2.

Fucking mirror image.

"Idiot!" he castigated himself.

But Spencer had rallied. He was on the board. Whatever happened, even if he lost the match, it wouldn't be to love.

Adrenaline raced through him. No way was Garrett not invested. He was invested to his eyeballs. Hell, to the crown of his scalp. No point not giving in, Garrett stepped down from the treadmill and wound his way through the gym to join two other guys watching the muted on-court action up close.

When Garrett got close enough, he recognised them as the Hargraves brothers—the British doubles pair who'd been riding high for years.

He ignored them and felt up the side of one of the flatscreens for the tell-tale control buttons, and the commentator's voices blared out.

"This is extraordinary, Aaron. Bloom faced three titans of the game on his way to the semi-finals—Javier, Anton, and Herc—but, here today, against Levi, he seems to have met his match. The local crowd will be devastated that the fairy tale is coming to an end."

"Don't write him off yet, Saheed. I've talked to this guy. We've seen him rally. He has fire in his eyes, and nothing to lose."

Nothing but his right to play.

The import of what he and Spencer had been up to in secret abruptly struck Garrett in the solar plexus.

Did he regret it?

No.

But, would he regret it if Spencer's exemplary record at the Queensland Championship Cup was tarnished because Ruth, or Toby, or any of the other tournament referees found out that he and Spencer couldn't keep their hands off of each other? Because Garrett couldn't control his desire?

Yes.

Yes, he would regret that.

Garrett knew how it felt to lose a bright future. He'd give just about anything to be back out there on the footy field, setting the tone for a fair fight.

His dream was over. Garrett couldn't do a thing about that. But he could do something for Spencer.

He could stop what they were doing before it was too late.

He could take a step back and set the man free.

God. Just the thought of it was a punch to the gut, but, win or lose, Garrett silently promised, he'd get out of Spencer's way.

"Bloom deserves to get his arse kicked," Jerome said in his plummy British accent. He didn't seem to give a shit if anyone heard him bagging Spencer.

"Don't be a twat, Jerome," said Callum, in his near-identical voice.

Jerome raised a brow and sneered, "I'm not the prick who left you in the lurch, Callum."

The pair stood there, both with their arms crossed, looking less that happy at what was unfolding on screen.

Garrett wasn't happy either, but he got the feeling it was for entirely different reasons.

"I told you," Callum said, "Spencer explained what happened. And it didn't matter in the end anyway."

"Yes, Callum, I know." Jerome punched a finger at the screen. "Because Mr. Perfect came along and whisked you—"

"He's not perfect. Stop saying that," Callum huffed.

"Not my fault you have a boner for Levi B—"

"Jerome! Shut. The fuck. Up."

Jerome smirked, "Fine. I get it. Levi helped you out in a time of need. That doesn't make him a hero. Just a *nice guy*." He didn't need to use his fingers to emphasis sarcasm, but Jerome was clearly a shithead who couldn't resist needling his brother.

"Thank you," Callum said with nearly as much sarcasm.

Silence descended for a few beats, then Jerome said, "But Bloom's still a prick."

"Hey!" Garrett couldn't listen to another word. "Mind yourself."

They turned to him so closely in sync it was creepy.

"Ah," Callum bit his lip. He looked like he was trying not to laugh. "Sorry for the French."

Jerome leaned sideways into his offsider and whispered *loud*, "Didn't think Aussies had such fucking tender ears." That earned him an elbow in the side.

"Apologies for my brother. He was dropped on his head—"

"Many times." Jerome grinned.

"—at birth."

Garrett didn't really give a shit if the dude had been dropped daily, so long as he stopped bad-mouthing Spencer.

He directed a glare Jerome's way.

Jerome glared back, looking far too happy with himself—as though causing shit was his number one hobby.

Callum didn't seem like quite so much of a bastard, so Garrett didn't have his defences up when he tilted his head quizzically and said, "Aren't you that umpire who got all up in Spencer's face? The foot-fault guy?"

Jerome gaped. "Holy shit. It is! What an arsehole."

Jesus. Was the guy defending Spencer now?

Jerome's swift change in sentiment practically gave Garrett whiplash.

What could he say in return? He was the foot-fault guy. He couldn't exactly protest against that truth. But it wasn't him that'd gotten in Spencer's face. It was the other way around. And neither brother needed to know anything about how they'd gotten in each other's faces, for real, since then.

Unable to say anything about that, Garrett pressed his lips together, hard, and doubled down on his glare.

Neither of them looked intimidated.

Callum's eyes narrowed. "For someone who just about killed Spencer's chances in the first round, you're awfully interested in his match today."

"Probably watching to see if he screws up again." Jerome waved lazily at the screen. "Be my guest."

Taking that as permission to ignore them both, Garrett turned back to the screen.

"Shit." Sometime in the sixty seconds since the two Brits distracted him, Spencer had lost his serve.

Since the only time Spencer had won a game was when Garrett wasn't watching, he considered turning his back on the television, but he just couldn't do it. Besides, he didn't believe in superstitions—lies people told themselves to try to get a sense of control over their lives. The only thing certain was the truth. Looking away wouldn't do a thing to help Spencer. So, he stayed. And he watched. Every excruciating point.

People around him came and went from the gym, but Garrett didn't pay them any attention. He'd found his line of focus—and that was the guy on the court above putting his heart and soul and grit into every fucking point.

Spencer put up a fight.

He did.

But it wasn't enough.

When it was over, Garrett silently switched down the volume, collected his knapsack, and made his way out of the gym to his sentinel post in the corridor.

The place hummed with activity.

Garrett supposed he ought to have been wary of being noticed, but, like anyone alone in a crowd, the mass of strangers seemed to render him anonymous.

It didn't take long for Spencer to come out. A long-sleeve zip-up top covered his sweat-dark t-shirt. His tennis bag dragged at his shoulder, looking like it weighed twice as much as usual. And, his poor man bun was still wonky, with so much hair hanging loose he looked more Muppet than man.

Garrett wasted half a second wondering where Spencer's oh-so-supportive coach was, then he tuned that out, too. It didn't matter where Kaz was...*he* was there. If all Spencer needed was to not have to lick his wounds on his own, Garrett would be there for him.

Before he left Brisbane, that was.

The heavy door shut behind Spencer and he looked up, directly to Garrett.

Suddenly, Garrett didn't give a shit about whether or not they were temporary, or keeping their connection secret, or any of the other rational reasons for keeping his hands to himself in public. Spencer was hurting. He needed Garrett. And the instinct to offer support overrode every reason to steer clear.

As if time slowed, the people moving between them became nothing but blurry ghosts, and Garrett was halfway across the corridor with his arms around Spencer before he could take a single breath.

"I'm all sweaty," Spencer protested.

"Don't care." Garrett wormed his hands between Spencer's bulky tennis bag and his sweat-hot back.

When Spencer returned the embrace, Garrett couldn't stop an empathetic shudder from rippling through him.

Spencer squeezed him tighter.

Painfully tight.

But Garrett didn't let go.

In synchrony, Spencer tucked his nose down to Garrett's ear, and Garrett lifted his chin to align the softest flesh of their cheeks. Garrett drew in a deep, calming breath, and, as he exhaled, he heard a corresponding release by his ear.

Ahh.

When Garrett breathed in again, Spencer inhaled too, and Garrett could feel it drawing deep into the base of their collective lungs.

God, it felt so good.

So right.

"What the fuck!" A far too familiar voice attacked from the side.

Shit!

Jerome Hargraves.

The wanker from the gym.

Spencer went stiff as a statue.

The world rushed in.

And Garrett instinctively leaped back.

Or, he tried to.

With Spencer's arms clamped tight around him, Garrett could barely shift an inch.

Thinking quickly, he gave Spencer a hearty slap on the meat of his shoulder. "Bad luck, mate," he said in an over-loud, over-compensating voice, then patted him again for good measure. Bro-hug style. "You did brilliant, though. Semi-final. Wowsers!" *Wowsers? Jesus, Fellows. What century are you from?* "You did so much better than we all expected."

At that, Spencer came back to life. He let go of Garrett and stepped away so fast Garrett had to grab onto an older stranger's arm for balance.

"Y'right mate?" the portly man jerked away.

"Sorry. So sorry." Garrett apologised blindly, since all his attention was on Spencer, and the Brit brothers, and the shithouse mistake he'd made.

But Spencer's attention wasn't on Garrett. "Fuck off, Jerome."

"Yeah, no, that's not going to happen." Jerome sneered.

"What are you doing with him?" Callum couldn't have looked more shocked.

"We're just..." Spencer's head swivelled, searching.

"Friends," Garrett offered.

It wasn't a lie, exactly. It just wasn't the whole truth. And nobody but him and Spencer owned that truth.

"Uh-hu." Callum obviously didn't believe him, but Garrett didn't give a fuck. He only cared what Spencer thought. How Spencer felt.

"Yeah, right." Jerome rapped his brother on the chest with his knuckles. "And he's my fucking aunt."

CHAPTER TWENTY-FIVE

Spencer

"Did you stand me up to be with him?" Callum blurted out. "The other day, when we were supposed to practice together."

"What? No."

Yes.

But it wasn't like that.

And where did Callum get off, sounding like a woman scorned?

They'd hooked up a few times over the years, and kept each other's secret, but it wasn't as though he owed Callum any kind of fealty.

The glower on Jerome's face was pretty stock standard.

The frown on Callum's face, however, was a surprise.

Alarm bells probably ought to have rung in Spencer's ears, but he couldn't deal with the Hargrave brothers. Not right then.

He'd rushed out of the stadium, needing to get away from all those faces—all those people he'd disappointed—and straight into Garrett's waiting arms.

Well done, mate. You did so much better than we all expected.

God. How Spencer hated expectations.

It had felt so good to let Garrett hold him up. Just for a while. But, the second those words were spoken, Spencer pulled back. The disappointment was too much. Especially on top of his epic semi-final failure. Coming from Garrett, they felt infinitely worse.

Meanwhile, Callum and Jerome were still waiting for an explanation.

What were he and Garrett to each other? He wasn't certain. All Spencer knew was how they'd gotten there.

"After the whole foot-fault…" he searched for the right word.

"Debacle," Garrett offered.

"Yeah. Good word. Thanks. After that, we had a…" his mind went blank again.

He heard Garrett clear his throat behind him. God. So close.

An awkward moment went by while Callum's eyes flickered between him and Garrett.

Garrett stepped up closer behind him. So close Spencer could feel the man's warmth.

"Professional discussion," Garrett finished for him again.

Spencer heaved out a breath. "Yep. Since then, we've become kinda, sorta…" Spencer's words dried up.

Help me out here, Garrett. I'm flailing.

"Friends."

Cheers, mate.

"We get together and talk about, ah…"

Jesus, Bloom, spit it out!

"Tennis," Garrett said.

Spencer gave a short, sharp nod in agreement.

"You're full of shit, Bloom." Jerome's eyes narrowed to slits. "You too, whatever the fuck your name is."

Garrett moved out from behind Spencer, brushing his side in the process, and stretched out his hand to shake. "Garrett. Garrett Fellows."

Spencer's right arm tingled with awareness. God, he'd give just about anything to re-start the day. Or, better yet, re-start from yesterday. At least then he could have woken less than a hair width away from Garrett.

Being on his best behaviour before his semi-final match had meant waking alone in the shiver-cold air-conditioning, followed by a warm up practice, followed by Kaz giving him the stink eye while telling him all the ways he needed to modify his game to have any hope of winning against Levi.

Yeah, no. Today is not a day to repeat.

Garrett nudged his elbow. "Right?"

"Huh?"

"Jerome here seems to think we're both full of shit."

And I care about that, why?

He probably should care what Jerome had to say. The man could create problems for both him and Garrett.

Correction—the man could expose the problem they'd already created for themselves.

Jerome wasn't any more to blame than Callum.

"This isn't right, Spencer. I expected better of you," Callum said in his snootiest tone.

As far as guilt trips went, it wasn't a ten-tonne block of cement, but Spencer felt it to his toes, because there was that word again—expectation.

No matter what he did, or how hard he tried, he'd never fulfil everyone's hopes and dreams and goddamn expectations. How could he when they were so much grander than even his own?

Sometimes it felt like nobody knew who he was at all. Garrett had come pretty close. In the short time they'd spent together, Spencer had felt seen. But those words on the man's tongue—*better than we all expected*—had him spooked.

Did everyone expect something from him?

Could nobody be happy with what he'd already achieved?

Appreciate him for who he already was?

Love him for—

Garrett stepped abruptly into the space between him and Callum. "Mate, you need to back off," he growled, his voice as serious and as uncompromising as Spencer had ever heard it.

Heat rushed through Spencer's body.

Fuck, Garrett was gorgeous.

In the private space between them, he clenched his hand in a fist, dragged his knuckles up over the swell of Garrett's arse, and lodged it in the concave curve above his hip. For a heartbeat, Garrett stilled. Rigid. Then Spencer felt him relax.

Over Garrett's shoulder, Spencer saw Callum's expression go from angry to suspicious to astonished to...delighted?

That can't be right.

Callum winked at him, which was just plain bewildering, then said, "Come on, Jerome. Let's leave these two bffs to it."

Jerome looked like he was about to protest, but Callum did that creepy silent communication thing doubles partners were so good at, not to mention brothers, then they turned and strode off to disappear into the swarm of people. It was as though they'd never even been there at all.

Obviously, Callum must have seen something in Garrett's expression for him to change his tune like that. But when he turned around, Spencer couldn't see it. "Do I wanna know what that was about?" Spencer asked.

Please answer 'no', please answer 'no'.

"Probably not."

Oh, thank you, Jesus.

"But we should probably talk," said Garrett.

Ugh. No. I do not *want to talk.*

All of a sudden, the weight of the day came crashing down on him. His body felt like lead and his brain like mush. All he wanted to do was shower, fall into bed, and hide himself away until a new day—a better day—began.

Spencer hiked up his heavy bag, turned, and began the short walk down the corridor to the security door that led to the tunnel to Tennyson Bend.

He couldn't have gone more than half a dozen steps before he felt a touch on his left shoulder and the weight of his bag was gone. "My swipe card's in there," he protested.

"I got it."

"But..."

"I got it," Garrett insisted in a rough voice.

And he did, for all of twenty more steps till they reached the heavy, fire-resistant door.

Garrett handed him the bag. "I can't go through there with you."

That made no sense. "You carried my bag, and walked me here, but you're not coming with me?" Maybe it was just the endorphin crash that made him unable to compute.

"Sorry." Garrett bit his lip.

Spencer's back stiffened. He dropped his bag to the floor and let the door swing shut without going through. "You're sorry. Why?"

Garrett's eyes shifted away. "Look, so long as those arseholes keep their mouths shut, and we say goodbye here, then you're in the clear."

"Clear of what?"

"Every time we're seen together, you risk your career."

"And you risk yours."

"This isn't about me."

Like hell it wasn't. "This is all about you. For fuck's sake, Garrett, we just embraced in the middle of the stadium corridor, surrounded by staff." His eyes blurred like he'd drunk three pints straight. God, he was tired. "We can deny there's something going on between us it 'til we're blue in the face, but if Jerome decides to speak out..." Shit. What then? "People know he's a hot-head, but he's not a liar."

"And what about your boy Callum?"

"Callum's not my anything."

"Yeah, right."

Spencer blinked. "He's not." Why was Garrett was acting like a jealous boyfriend? "Callum's a friend."

"Uh-hu. Word of the day." Garrett muttered.

What the hell was Garrett's problem? "We said we'd give this thing between us a go." Spencer hated how small his voice sounded—so weak; so wishful.

"We also said it was temporary," Garrett said, dry as toast.

Spencer reared back. How could that simple truth feel like such a punch to the gut?

"And you choose now to call it quits? Here?" Spencer waved his arm at the people that milled about. It wasn't likely that anyone could hear them, but breaking off a relationship in public was the coward's way out. Even he knew that.

After the walloping he'd taken on court, Spencer's skin felt paper thin. He wasn't sure if he could take another loss. But if who he was didn't meet Garrett's needs, or wants, or fucking expectations, then...well...Garrett Fellows could fuck right off.

The only loss was the pressure to be someone he wasn't, and he'd already received more than enough of that.

So what if he craved Garrett's arms around him.

He'd be fine on his own.

He always had been.

Spencer heaved in a giant breath. "I don't need this right now."

"I'm just trying to protect you." Garrett looked earnest—like he believed his own false justification. "It's not like this was ever going to be something real. This thing," he waved his hand between them, "was never part of your game-plan."

Spencer brushed that off.

It didn't matter what the man said.

The only true thing was they were done.

"You're right," Spencer said, because he'd already battled enough for one day. If he was so much of a loser that Garrett wasn't willing to fight for them, then Spencer wouldn't either. "Better to stop now before we get in any deeper."

Garrett nodded. "Yeah. Okay. Good."

"Excellent."

Spencer didn't wait for further confirmation. He'd be damned if he'd give any more energy to Garrett fucking Fellows. He hefted his bag with muscles that felt like jelly, swiped the lock open, and leaned all his weight into the heavy door.

If he took one long glance back before he let it shut with a solid thud behind him, well...sue him...Spencer hadn't ever met anyone who'd rocked his world quite like Garrett. And, from the look on the man's face as the gap in the closing door narrowed to nothing, Garrett was fooling himself if he thought what he felt was anything less than real, too.

A twinge of regret flickered in his heart, but it was too late to back-track on anything said—any hurt he may have inflicted.

"More fool you," he said to the back of the steel door, not too sure if it was himself or Garrett he was addressing. Then he turned and retreated home.

CHAPTER TWENTY-SIX

Garrett

The minute the security door slammed shut with him on one side and Spencer on the other, Garrett knew he'd made a mistake.

Not a total mistake. Spencer would almost certainly be better off going forward without Garrett's deadweight hanging on. And given how quick Spencer had been to lie to the Brit brothers, saying that they were nothing more than friends before he up-tailed and ran away, Garrett was pretty sure he was also right to call it quits. Not all that had gone on between them had been a lie, but Spencer clearly felt less for him than he felt for Spencer. He was better off in the long run without that heartbreak.

But that was long-term thinking.

It didn't help him feel any better in the moment, and it sure didn't help him look forward to day's end when he'd have nowhere to go but the sterile guest room in Toby and Hamish's house. Alone.

Garrett rubbed the centre of his chest, right over the spot where Spencer had habitually laid his hand.

"Jerome got it right," he said to the blank door. "We're both full of shit."

It was done, though, and Garrett had to put it behind him.

So, he returned to the gym. He diligently completed all the stretches and exercises Kevin had mapped out for his recovery. Then he slowly walked the winding suburban streets along the Brisbane River, through the muggy summer evening, to Toby and Hamish's townhouse. He let himself in through the front door, waved off Hamish's friendly offering of a glass of red, and retreated to the quiet of the guest suite. A shower and his hand would be all the comfort he'd get that night before starting all over again the next day, when, as luck would have it, Ruth assigned his gamma crew to call the shots on Saturday's men's doubles final.

Garrett couldn't have planned it worse if he'd tried.

At one end of the court were two perfectly reasonable players from Morocco and Spain. At the other end were the brothers Hargraves.

He'd thought about fessing up to Ruth the moment he got his assignment on Saturday morning. To tell her that he'd have a hard time staying unbiased against the pair. But his minor conflict of interest with the British brothers was so closely related to his much larger conflict of interest with Spencer that he felt forced to tamp down his disquiet and stay mute.

Of course, when Callum and Jerome arrived on court and spied him, looks could kill. Every 'out' call and 'in' sign he made were met with hostility on Jerome's part and suspicion on Callum's, so constant that Garrett started second-guessing himself.

Doubt.

It was the bane of a referee's job.

In truth, the shots made on court weren't the only thing he was doubting. His whole life felt like shifting clay. But he stuck it out. "Keep it simple, stupid," he reminded himself as he rotated with the rest of gamma crew from line to line.

Each point a battle. One at a time. He called as he saw it.

In or out.

Win or loss.

Right or wrong.

The attitudes and opinions of the players on court didn't matter. All that mattered was the ball and the line. And as the tight match went on, Garrett lost himself in the clarity of each given moment. The face of the four athletes disappeared in a blur of action, his doubt fizzled away, and what remained was his skill, his certainty, and the solid blue court beneath his feet.

This I can count on, Garrett thought as he brought his hands together on the final point to indicate the ball was in.

When he looked up to see the Hargraves brothers, mid-court, celebrating their win with a heartfelt, joyous embrace, Garrett knew, absolutely, what cold comfort felt like. Because right then, the certainty he'd felt in pushing Spencer away evaporated.

As soon as he got off court, Toby was there, looking frazzled. "What was all that about?"

Garrett shook his head. "Nothing."

Toby pointed back through the opening to the wide expanse of the court. "That wasn't nothing. Jerome Hargraves is a piece of work, but he's usually better behaved with officials. And

Callum. I've never seen him stare down calls like that. I almost had Ruth pull you out."

"Sorry."

"Geez, don't be sorry, mate. You were brilliant. Like ice. Stoic to the core."

"Oh. Thanks." How could Toby complement him for the least professional referee job he'd ever done? And he couldn't even tell his friend why. Clearly, the only way to avoid further deception was to take his lying self not just out of Spencer's life, but out of the equation altogether.

Garrett shoved his hands into his uniform pockets. "Look, would you be cool if I took off tonight?"

"Sure. Hamish won't be expecting you for dinner, but I can send him a quick text. He won't mind cooking two steaks instead of one."

"No. I mean...fly back home. To Melbourne. Ruth already confirmed that I won't be needed for the men's final tomorrow. Not much point me sticking around any longer if I'm not needed." Not for his heart, anyway.

And he'd be too far away to screw up Spencer's life any more than he already had.

"Oh. Okay." A frown pinched between Toby's brows. "I was hoping we could have a proper catch up once we're done here. I won't be free till late tomorrow, but..." He must have seen something in Garrett's expression, because he paused and settled back on his heels. "But if you need to go. Of course. I understand. But, ah...expect a phone call from me soon." He flashed a quick look around and lowered his voice. "You didn't hear it from me, but once this tournament is done and dusted, I'll be forming the referee committee for the Olympic Games."

"The Brisbane Olympics? But that's years away."

"Not really. Planning starts early, and I want you on board."

"Me?" Stunned, Garrett's voice rose embarrassingly high.

"You're not tied to any one sport," Toby said, which made Garrett wince. He *had* been tied to AFL. Past tense. His future, though, was less certain.

Toby went on. "I'm sorry, but it's true. And you're all the more valuable for it. You're a stellar referee, Garrett, across far more fields than footy."

Garrett's eyebrows rise at that claim. "Stellar?"

It was Toby's turn to wince. "Well, maybe there have been a few less-than-stellar moments during this tournament, but it's not just tennis I need help with. I'll be in charge of finding the officials for the entire Games. I know what we need on paper, but you know what's needed on the ground. We'll be a perfect team."

Perfect. Was there such a thing?

"Anyway. I've got to go, but think about it." Toby waggled his thumb and pinkie beside his ear in the universal 'I'll call you' gesture, then raced away.

Garrett blinked. Stunned into stillness.

He probably ought to have been excited about Toby's offer, Garrett thought, but all he could think about was Spencer as he collapsed into his window seat on the last flight to Melbourne, and then as he closed his eyes against the bright freeway lights during the witching hour taxi ride home from the airport.

By the time he shut the door on his apartment, his hips and knees felt like they'd been fused at ninety-degree angles and he thought far too seriously about waking Kevin up in the dead of night for a deep tissue massage.

His dreams were a weird mishmash of Kevin and Spencer doing all sorts of oh-so-good and not-so-good things to his body, and when he woke up to the white glare of day, his body didn't seem to know if it felt horny or hurt.

"Ugh. Both."

Garrett palmed his morning wood and gave it a dry tug, but his heart really wasn't in it, and the need to piss soon overtook those concerns.

After a blistering hot shower, Garrett charged his favourite coffee mug, found the television remote stuck in the arse crack of his sofa, and sat down in his usual spot. Just as he raised the remote to power up the screen, he saw his shadowy reflection in the black glass and stilled.

Scarcely a week had passed since he'd flown to Brisbane, but he looked like a whole different man. Gone was the sad sack who'd barely been able to get off the sofa. He barely recognised himself with the square-set shoulders and head held high.

"Life's shit," he said to his shadowy reflection in the television screen—testing the words.

Objectively, the claim was still true.

His body no longer worked the way it should. His career was still an anaemic pile of shit. And he'd lost Spencer.

No. That wasn't right. He hadn't lost Spencer. Garrett had given up on having him, because...

Because, why?

Because Spencer deserved better?

Better than someone who's career was on the skids. Even though, if Toby was to be believed, those prospects looked brighter by the day.

Because he didn't trust Spencer with his heart?

Spencer had been quick to leave, with very little push. But it was Garret who'd provided that push.

Because he was afraid?

That thought stopped Garrett in his tracks.

Was he afraid?

Garrett peered up and took a long, hard look at his dark reflection.

This was about him. He'd pushed Spencer away. He'd run scared. He'd let fear win.

Garrett placed his hand flat to the middle of his chest and heard the heavy pulse of his heart pounding in his ears.

What was he so afraid of?

Scared to dream? Scared to offer his heart? Scared to lose it?

He'd thought he was done with all that victim mentality bullshit.

"Screw that," Garrett told himself.

Time to face reality, Fellows.

The only path to sure failure was to do nothing.

Risk nothing.

What he had was a simple binary choice—action or inaction.

He dropped the remote on the coffee table beside his half-drunk brew, pushed himself off the sofa, unplugged his phone from its charger, and scrolled through his contacts for Kevin's number.

"Mate," Kevin answered in his ridiculously cheerful voice.

"Hey Kev. How goes it?"

"Garrett, my man. Are you back from the super-sunny Sunshine State?"

"Yeah. Can you fit me in? I'm in dire need of a dose of your magic."

"Magic, eh? That's a turnaround. Last I heard you said I'm evil." He cackled an evil laugh for a few seconds, then said, "Hang on a sec. Let me just..."

Garrett heard a thud, then a rustling of papers, and a woman's laughter, and he wondered just what he'd interrupted at, "Oh, shit," not quite six o'clock on a Sunday morning.

"Sorry Kev!" he yelled through the phone in his best referee voice, "I'll call you back tomorr—!"

"Damn, G, nothing wrong with those vocal cords."

"Oops. Sorry. I was just saying—"

"Yeah, yeah. I heard you loud and clear. It's no worries. Can you get here in about an hour?"

Thank you, Jesus.

Garrett eyed the time. He'd have to hustle. "I'll be there," he promised.

Any potential of a life with Spencer might be gone, but that didn't mean every hope was dashed. He could take control of his recovery, and his career—however that looked.

An hour later, Garrett set off the jangling bells on the front door of Kevin's physio studio and approached the deserted receptionist's desk.

"G?" Kevin called from somewhere in the back.

"It's me."

"Great. Come on through."

Garrett did just that.

"Wow! You look amazing! What did you do? I bet it's the Queensland sun—miraculous vitamin D—and the ocean air. Now we know what to do the next time you're in the doldrums."

"What's that?"

"Go north, of course!"

Garrett rolled his eyes. "It's summer down here, too, you know Kev. We have the sun, and ocean, and," he couldn't resist adding, "air."

Kevin waved Garrett's lame joke off and patted a large, inflated yoga ball. "Come sit. Tell Kev absolutely everything."

And he did. Though not *absolutely* everything. Garrett kept Spencer's identity to himself, and glossed over the racier details of their time together. Which left a surprising amount left to tell.

The sex had been great, but what he really missed were Spencer's quirks and the quiet times together. For all their secrets, he'd felt a total lack of artifice in Spencer's company. In the telling, he realised what an idiot he'd been for not seeing that Spencer knew his own mind. Spencer was a grown man, capable of making his own decisions, his own mistakes, and pursuing his own dreams. And, for a while at least, those dreams had included Garrett—scars and all.

Had being the operative word.

"So, now I'm home," Garrett summed up, "And I'm going to need your help."

He'd never be able to leap tall buildings for his man, but if he could rehabilitate his body well enough to be able to leap tall boulders, that might just rate him worthy of his beautiful Achilles.

Chapter Twenty-Seven

Spencer

"I'm so glad that's all over. It's exhausting!" Lachlan collapsed dramatically on Spencer's sofa.

"What? Me losing?"

"And winning. Watching you compete is awfully stressful, Spencer."

"Well, you're going to have to cope with more, because I'm off to Melbourne for the Australian Open." Spencer tried to keep his voice steady and neutral. Inside, he was anything but steady, and there was nothing neutral about his feelings.

"Serious?!" Lachlan jack-knifed up.

"Yep." His gut turned, remembering the events as they occurred when the email arrived. Kaz had given him a pass on Sunday, but Monday morning practice was a different story.

He'd dragged his feet, shot daggers at his coach for no good reason whatsoever, and framed every second ball. Kaz seemed convinced it was just the deflation following his semi-final loss, but Spencer knew better.

When the email came through from the Australia Open, Kaz had crowed, and Spencer had been…glad.

He had.

Entry to the AO was a major win. The wildcard ought to have made it his best day ever. But Spencer couldn't seem to shake himself free of the doldrums after the proverbial punch in the gut Garrett had delivered forty-two-and-a-half hours before—not that he was counting or anything.

Enter Lachlan and a six-pack of beer.

Spencer flicked through his phone app and flashed the email with the AO logo in front of Lachlan's face. "See. Wildcard offered and accepted."

"That's awesome." He grabbed the phone from Spencer's hand and scrolled through. "Congrats, man. Wait, let me get Brady down here. He needs in on this." Lachlan whipped out his own phone and thumbed it, rapid-fire. He waited a few seconds, then came an answering ding. "He'll be here in a few."

"Awesome," Spencer's repeated his friend's word in an apathetic monotone.

Lachlan unlatched Spencer's front door before retaking his place on the sofa. "Wait, that's why you wanted beer? I thought you said you said you needed a shoulder to cry on."

"That's not what I said."

"You said, and I quote, 'Lachy, I need you. Bring beer.' That's a desperate cry for shoulder-time if ever I heard it."

"Hmph." Had he really sounded that pathetic?

Yes. Yes, you did. And you need to get over it.

Spencer couldn't think of anything to say that wouldn't make him sound like a whiney idiot, so he took a long slug of his beer then clamped his mouth shut.

Lachlan, on the other hand, who couldn't keep his mouth shut at the best of times, asked, "So...how's it going with your guy?"

Spencer shook his head. "Not my guy."

"Fine, your *hypothetical* guy."

"Ugh. No...I mean..." Spencer gave up, because it felt shitty to admit that Garrett wasn't his guy...not any more...never really had been. Maybe. Spencer hadn't managed to untangle everything that had been said and unsaid in Garrett's unexpected goodbye. Wrapped up in the massive disappointment of his loss in the Queensland Championship Cup, Spencer wasn't sure that he could trust his recollection. It just didn't jive with the rest of his memories of Garrett and the time they'd spent together.

Since that version of reality was a confusing miasma, he'd taken to dreaming up what ifs—the land of hypotheticals.

In his favourite, Garrett had been a victim of circumstances, too. He'd been acting the hero. Taking one for their two-man team.

It wasn't exactly a what-if Spencer wanted to wallow in, but it was the most plausible of them all, and it made Spencer feel a tiny bit less angry, less hurt, and less convinced that Garrett hadn't known him at all.

He eyed his friend. Lachlan was a primary school teacher. He was used to kids and their parents making stuff up. With any luck, he wouldn't laugh in Spencer's face if he floated his best what if out loud. Would he?

Worth a try, Bloom.

"So, hypothetically, if a guy dumps you in order to protect you, what's the best course of action? A. Hide in a hole and never come out. B. Hide in a hole, but come back out when you realise that you're an idiot not to have figured out earlier that he was probably only trying to protect his own heart when he crushed yours like a bug beneath his shoe. Or, C. Kidnap said man, hide together in a hole, and never come out, ever again."

"Oh, cool. A quiz. I like those." Lachlan lay back down on the two-seater sofa, with his feet hanging off the end, and stared up at Spencer's ceiling to think.

Spencer tried to do the same, but on a single seater it was tricky, and he didn't find any helpful wisdom in the bland white paint. After about ten seconds, he got impatient. "So, hypothetically, what would you do...hypothetically?"

"Can I have a D option?"

"Dick?" Spencer asked, surprised. He'd never heard Lachlan discuss his love-life—or lack thereof. "That's kinda included in option C."

"No, I mean a fourth option—for those of us who don't really do the 'hole' thing." Lachlan air-quoted, his beer bottle waving dangerously above his head. "Pun intended."

Spencer thought about that escape clause for about a quarter of a second. "Nope."

"Hmm. Okay, then. Well...for lack of a D option, *I* hypothetically choose B, because at least there's a way out of the hypothetical hole, *and* his hypothetical angst can go fuck itself, *and* we can all get on with more important things like figuring out how to set hypothetical you up as the protector of his hypothetical heart, rather than making hypothetical him have to protect his hypothetical heart from hypothetical you...if you know what I mean. Hypothetically."

Spencer blinked.

"But we're not talking about hypothetical me here, we're talking about hypothetical you, who is a different hypothetical entirely."

Spencer's brain hurt. "I'm really regretting this conversation."

There was a knock at Spencer's front door and it swung open.

Lachlan went on, "To sum up, you're an idiot. Hypothetically."

Brady strolled in, jangling his keys in his hand. "Who's an idiot?"

"Our boy Spencer."

"What did he do this time?" Brady asked.

"Hey!" *Geez.* "With friends like these," Spencer muttered.

Lachlan ignored him. "What took you so long?" he asked Brady.

Brady pointed his thumb over his shoulder. "Had a visitor." He blushed, hard. He tried to cover it as he went to Spencer's fridge, came back with a beer, lifted Lachlan's legs up, and flopped down underneath them on the couch, but Spencer and Lachlan knew him too well.

"Oh-ho!" Lachlan cried. "Do tell."

Spencer sighed. It was a relief to have the attention off of him and his situation. "Jesus, Lachy. For an ace guy, you sure are a sucker for romance."

"Truth," Brady concurred.

"Hey!" Lachlan protested at the ribbing.

Brady patted Lachlan's legs. "This guy's asexual, not aromantic, which explains the secret stash of Jane Austen novels I found under his bed."

"And *maybe* he's just private," Lachlan grumped.

Spencer and Brady both look at him, and burst out laughing. "Yeah, no," they both said.

"You're arseholes. Why do I even hang out with you guys?"

"Because we're awesome," Brady hovered his hand over the coffee table for a distant high-five, which Spencer gave back.

"Because you love us," Spencer added.

"Yeah, right. Must've forgotten that amongst all the gasbagging about my sexuality."

"Must've," Brady agreed.

Spencer surveyed the two of them, lolled on his sofa like a couple of degenerate cats. His third beer had finally gone to his head, and all seemed well. "I love you guys."

He heard the clink of Brady and Lachlan's bottle necks knocking together, but Spencer's attention had strayed from his friends. His mind had gone back to the last time he'd felt so relaxed and free to be himself—to when he and Garrett had lazed in bed, doing nothing but talking and touching and tasting. The warmth and the thrill, simmering in his veins. He'd never felt anything quite like it. Not even winning on centre court had felt so good.

"I love him," Spencer realised.

"Yep," said Lachlan.

"Who?" Brady asked.

"And I need to figure out a way to get him back."

"Hallelujah." Lachlan raised his bottle. "Nothing hypothetical about that."

Chapter Twenty-Eight

Spencer

Christina Gates, Aussie champ from the classic era of the game, wasn't the most intimidating person to face in an interview, but Spencer's heart still raced a mile a minute.

"Congratulations, Spencer. That was an astonishing win on your first tilt at the Australian Open. How does it feel?" she asked.

How does it feel?

Déjà vu, was his first thought. A few weeks had gone by since his first-round win in Brisbane, but it was like he was back there all over again. Aside from the slight chill in the dry southern air, and the magnified scale of the complex at Melbourne Park compared to Brisbane's tennis centre, the moment was almost a carbon copy.

Again, he was the surprise winner of the first round against a superior player. And, again, he stood on the service line with a microphone at his chin, mind spinning, madly trying to think of something sensible and real and true to say.

In his mind's eye, Spencer could already see what he'd write on the day's calendar square:

AO 1ˢᵗ round

Spencer Bloom (99) v Shawn O'Connell (12) – WIN!

An achievement, for sure. One very few people attained. But that'd be it—a solo win in a square box. Nothing romantic about it.

Stalling for time, Spencer did a three-sixty to scan the audience for probably the thousandth time since he'd stepped foot on court that day. Was Garrett there? Had he seen him win? Spencer looked up to the near-cloudless blue summer sky. Were they sharing the same patch of the atmosphere, too?

He swatted at the sweaty strands of hair that had fallen from his fucking man bun and shoved them behind his ears, planted his hands on his hips, inhaled deep, and re-asked himself Christina's question. *How does it truly feel?* Answering that was easy...and really fucking hard, because the truth was heavy.

Spit it out, Bloom. This is what you're really here to do.

"It's a dream come true, you know, to be out here. Finally!" That got a happy round of applause. "It's crazy and wonderful and unexpected and...and lonely."

Oh, fuck. Why did you say that, Bloom?

Because it's true.

"Ugh." He exhaled heavily into the microphone, sending reverberations around the arena.

"Lonely?" Christina asked—because of course she'd pick up on that.

Like you gave her any other choice, Bloom.

She did that awful thing where she waited for him to answer the question.

Then she waited some more.

He wasn't ready, goddammit!

Yes, you are.

Spencer took a few seconds to re-gather his thoughts, then cleared his throat. "Career-wise, I'm at fifteen-love, I have everything ahead of me. I'm living the dream, you know? Half the year on the road playing the game that I love. But it's just me. I don't even have anyone in my player's box." His whole body clenched, but it was too late to contain the vulnerable admission—to put it in a heavy wooden pirate chest and shut the lid, tight.

Then he realised the mistake he'd made and he waved an apology to his player's box. "Except my coach, of course. Sorry, Kaz. Love you, man." Spencer's ears were buzzing so loud with nerves that the audience's laughter sounded canned.

Christine waited for the crowd to settle, then she asked, "And off court? Do you have someone you can rely on out there?"

"Ha! That's the rub, right?" He took a half step back from the microphone, then forward again, with intent. But the words wouldn't come.

Buck up, Spencer! This is what you're here for. Stick to the plan.

He gathered up more bravery than it had taken to walk out on centre court three hours earlier, and said, "Yeah. Yeah, I do. Sort of. Maybe."

"Oh?" Christine asked. Her voice was friendly, and light, and not at all demanding of an answer.

Spencer swallowed down the lump in his throat. "Garrett."

Oh, God! Oh, God! What have I done?

His thoughts rushed in a torrent. The only bit of him that wasn't a shaking mess was his heart. But it felt right, god-dammit. One-hundred percent right.

"Garrett?" Christine asked, and having tipped his hand, he couldn't put the truth back in the proverbial genie bottle.

He had to finish.

Spencer eyeballed one of the television cameras, licked the salt from his dry lower lip, and said, "If you're up for it, there's half a doubles court with your name on it."

"Oh, you mean a tennis partner?" Christine chuckled.

When she said nothing more, Spencer realised it was again his turn.

Shit! No going back now, Bloom.

The rally had already started.

Position your feet. Find your grip. Hit through the ball.

He re-focused on the camera lens. Took his stance. And went for it.

"I don't care about the perfect game plan, Garrett. All I care about is getting to deuce with you."

The next afternoon, Spencer's inner stoic was getting a serious workout, made even more serious when he got the news that the AO organisers had rejigged the schedule to set his second-round match on Rod Laver Arena—the biggest tennis stage in the nation. Which was a surprise. He'd expected to be either shuffled off to outer Siberia or for the tournament organizers to haul his arse in for questioning about the nature of his relationship with a tennis official.

Of course, the media was all over *that,* too.

After the three-dozenth call from a random journalist asking him about his 'special relationship with an umpire', Kaz had stolen his phone, said, "First comes tennis," then shoved a massive bowl of chicken cacciatore under his nose.

The second surprise was the support from the audience.

Even before he'd arrived on court, he could hear their roar.

The moment he walked out he saw hundreds of individuals speckled throughout the crowd decked out in every version of pride he could imagine. They whistled and cheered and waved rainbow flags.

Spencer was used to spectators, but never in his wildest dreams did he expect so many people to support him with such open enthusiasm.

It was...surreal.

His pathway to his player's chair was a meandering one as he spun this way and that—taking it all in.

Wishing.

Hoping.

That somewhere in the whirlwind was...

He stopped, mid-stride.

Garrett.

In his player's box.

He's here!

"You're here." Spencer's words were swallowed instantaneously.

Bright lights flickered at the side of Spencer's vision, and the noise of the crowd became an indistinct roar that blurred into the background as every bit of his attention honed in on Garrett.

Time slowed.

And while Spencer gaped, rivetted, Garrett lifted his hand and placed it flat to the centre of his chest.

His own hand twitched in response.

That was Spencer's hand. Spencer's habit. Spencer's way of connecting.

Garrett wasn't lying naked in Spencer's bed in Tennyson Bend, but he might as well have been, given how clearly Spencer could feel the whirls of chest hair against his fingers and palm. It was all memory. He knew that. But he could practically smell the vanilla and hazelnuts in the air.

He had to get up there.

He had to know...Jesus, he knew nothing!

But, the match, Spencer.

No way could he play a point, let alone an entire tennis match, without knowing what Garrett's presence meant for him...for them.

For us.

A surge of adrenaline gave his feet wings as he spun around, threw his towel and bag on his player's bench and hot-footed it to the base of the chair umpire's elevated seat.

The metal edge of the ladder up to the umpire's seat threatened to cut into his hand, he gripped it so tight. "I have to get up to him."

With or without permission, he'd be up in those stands.

Settle down, Bloom.

Breathe.

Exercise an iota of patience.

You can wait five seconds if it means not screwing up your AO campaign.

"Please." He added in a rush.

By all accounts, Raymond Clare was a decent guy. A good umpire. A fair man. But Spencer didn't know him well enough to identify if the man's flat expression was a good sign or not.

Was he gearing up to argue the rules? Or trying to keep a straight face?

Spencer didn't know.

He didn't know a whole hell of a lot, and his hard-won patience was wearing thin.

Then Raymond pushed his mounted computer tablet away and leaned forward over the front of his chair.

He gave a subtle chin-tilt in the direction of Spencer's box and kept his voice low as he said, "Go get him, Bloom."

It was all the permission Spencer needed.

To a chorus of wolf-whistles, and Raymond's ultra-professional voice emanating from the speakers, saying, "Mr. Bloom has requested a personal time out. Play will begin in five minutes," Spencer raced across the court to the flat-board front of the stands where he stretched to reach Garrett's open hand.

"Get up here, caveman," was Garrett's gruff valentine, eyes full of laughter and...God, Spencer hoped, more.

He dove sideways through the posse of court-side photographers, all snapping pictures and yelling, "look here, Spencer!", straddled his legs over the front boards into the lowest stands, and pressed on anonymous heads as he climbed up, up, up. The second he was there, Garrett pulled him over the last barrier, wrapped him tight in his arms, and, instantly, Spencer felt the calm descend inside their human cave of two.

He pressed his nose into Garrett's hair to breathe him in, and heard Garrett whisper, "I'm a craptastic arsehole, and I'm sorry. I'm so sorry."

"It's okay," he whispered back.

He didn't think Garrett heard him at first, then Garrett ever so slightly loosened his hold and leaned far enough back for Spencer to be able to read his earnest expression. "This isn't a fucking crush," he said, "Can we please forget short-term, temporary, over-before-you-know-it blips?"

Spencer knew his answer before Garrett had even finished his question. "Yes."

Hell, yes.

Always yes.

Stroking down the centre of Garrett's back, Spencer felt the ripple of scars under the rough cotton of his shirt. At the final, gentle curve, he spread his fingers wide and held on to as much ground as he could—staking his claim.

Perhaps, he thought, he ought to take Garrett to task for putting them both through purgatory, but they could hash all that out later. Right then, in that moment, all Spencer wanted to do was hold on tight.

He closed the gap and into Garrett's ear, he asked, "How are you here?"

"I got your message." The feel of Garrett's voice rumbling through Spencer's chest was near as good as skin on skin.

Almost.

"Yeah?"

"And I, ah…told Toby about us. About everything."

Spencer pulled back just enough to see Garrett's gorgeous face. "Everything?"

"Well…not absolutely everything." His face flamed. "But nearly. Enough to come clean. Enough to get Kaz's number. Enough to get—"

"Our help." Lachlan appeared out of nowhere, with Callum at his shoulder. Giant grins spread across their faces.

Stunned, Spencer sought out Kaz. He could understand Lachlan lending a hand. And Callum was already in Melbourne for the Open. But Kaz? "You helped?" Maybe his coach really was on his side.

Kaz held both hands out. "Happy player. Happy tennis."

Spencer saw straight through him. "You're a good man, Ivan Kazimov." He would've wrapped his coach up in a hug if his arms weren't already full. The 'aw shucks' look Kaz gave him in return was just a bonus.

Question upon question raced in his mind but he couldn't help repeating Garrett's own words—asking the one he'd left unanswered since he'd let Garrett walk away. "You'll come along for the ride?"

Quick on it, Garrett breathed out, "Of course."

There was no 'of course' about it. None of their history together had been 'of course'. But Spencer's heart wilfully ignored that minor fact.

Lachlan pushed at his shoulder. "Don't you think it's about time you unhand your man and go show us what you can do down there?"

"Clock's ticking, Bloom." Callum added his ounce of help.

Garrett loosened his hold. "Go, Spencer."

"Don't wanna," Spencer couldn't let go yet—not after the way he'd let that heavy door close firm between them.

"Do your thing." Garrett encouraged. "Play your heart out."

A golf ball lodged in Spencer's throat. He couldn't go until he'd made his position one-hundred percent clear. "No. I'll play my guts out, but my heart's already taken."

"Oh, my God." Lachlan groaned.

Callum burst with a fake cough, "Cheese!"

Spencer ignored them both.

Garrett wet his lower lip, and his nostrils flared. "Just one thing," he said, a gleam in his eye.

Oh shit! Oh shit! This is it!

"What's that?"

"No matter what, always remember to keep it simple—"

"Stupid," Spencer punctuated the line with a very un-sexy sniff.

"Nu-hu." Garrett disagreed. "We're changing that."

"To what?"

Garrett reached up to Spencer's man bun and pulled him closer. Forehead to forehead. "Keep it simple, sexy."

Boom! The sound shuddered so loud in his mind that it shook the rafters of his own personal arena.

Unable to resist another second, Spencer leaned in and laid a kiss on Garrett worthy of *Casablanca*, clear for the whole world to see.

EPILOGUE

Garrett

Three weeks later...

"Don't you ever use the facilities to shower?" Garrett asked as Spencer followed a security guard out of the door marked *Player's Facilities*. "Every time I meet you after a match you're dripping with sweat."

Spencer pointed back through the doorway. "I could go back if you like. Rinse off. Hang out with Kaz for a bit. Chug down some electrolytes. Or..."

"Or?" Something told Garrett he knew what the 'or' would be. He was on board with 'or'.

"*Or* you could help me shower. Get me re-eeal clean."

Yep. That was it.

"Callum was right about you."

Spencer raised a brow in question.

"The cheese. I don't know how I missed it."

Spencer huffed. "I'll have to do something about that."

"Why? I like it. Makes you unique." Not that Spencer wouldn't be unique without it—he was unlike anyone Garrett had ever met before.

"What's unique about cheese?"

"Special, then." Garrett ventured.

The other eyebrow went up.

"Interesting?"

"Try again, Mr. Fellows."

He checked to make sure the guard was out of hearing range. "Gorgeous?"

"Hmm."

"Talented?"

Spencer winced. "Try again."

"Mine?"

Spencer nodded. "Better."

Garrett felt the final whisp of tension he'd carried since the moment he'd called it quits on Spencer unravel.

He sighed.

They still had a lot to figure out, but the past was done, and Spencer had invited Garrett to share his future. In the waves of noise emanating from the massive arena beside them, he heard the ghost of Spencer's cryptic invitation.

All I care about is getting to deuce with you.

Spencer's life was tennis. If he wanted to share his doubles court, then Garrett was all for it.

"So..." Spencer fiddled with the strap of his tennis bag, "The Aussie Open has volunteer drivers. You ready to take a ride?" he asked.

Garrett had to laugh. He was ready and raring to go. And, as soon as they were somewhere private, he'd get Spencer to ride him for real.

"What's so funny?"

He shook his head. "Nothing. Come on, you." Garrett stepped up to walk beside Spencer as the guard led them away.

"I feel like I'm being escorted off the premises. I am allowed to be here, you know. Unless you got me into even more trouble than I probably am with the tennis gods."

"The tennis gods? Who are they?"

"Oh, you know..." Spencer waved his left arm in a wild backhand, just about whacking the security guard who actually was escorting Spencer off the premises. "Oops, sorry mate."

"No worries, Mr. Bloom."

"God. Don't start that Mr Bloom crap." He stuck his hand out to shake. "Spencer, please."

"Rune. Rune Coventry. Congratulations on your win tonight."

"You saw it?"

"Bits and pieces. A long match."

"Ha! I'll try to win quicker next time. Just for you."

Rune unsuccessfully hid a smile. "Much obliged."

"No worries. Hey, you don't happen to know who's behind the wheel tonight, do you? We're in a bit of a rush."

"Ah, well—"

"Because we have a date."

"We do?" That was news to Garrett. But when he saw Spencer's falling expression, he regrouped. "Right. Yeah. We do. We're going to..." his mind went blank.

Shit. Where would Spencer want to go on a date?

"To your place, remember? So that we can do that thing."

The thought of Spencer in his home...in his bed...in his... "Yes. Yes. That thing."

Rune gave a non-committal, "Mm-hmm," and walked a little faster.

Garrett tried to keep up with the both of them as they hustled to the waiting car emblazoned with the AO symbol and an action shot of Shawn O'Connell—ranked number twelve in the world—the player Spencer just beat.

Garrett was used to working alongside high profile sports stars, but the sight of Spencer's doppelganger on that car door was surreal. Give it another year, and his Achilles could be there.

The thought filled him with pride.

Is this my life? He wanted to ask the universe.

Garrett felt Spencer's step hitch as he noticed the image on the car, but that was his only reaction as he dropped Garrett's hand, threw his bag across the back seat of the car and slid in after it, head first. "Come on, Garrett."

Spencer Bloom was done wasting time.

"Where to, Mr Bloom?" The driver asked as they both clicked their seat belts in place.

"How far is it to your place?" Spencer asked.

Garrett checked his watch. "Ten, fifteen minutes if there's traffic. Why?"

"Because that's how long we've got to figure out how this relationship will work."

Garrett didn't need fifteen seconds to decide that he was committed, let alone fifteen minutes. Still, the logistics of their relationship would take longer than that to sort out. "Why the rush?"

Spencer's teeth gleamed in the near darkness. "Because once I've got you alone, there'll be no going back."

"Hmm…a fait accompli?" Garrett liked the sound of that. He curled a proprietary hand around Spencer's thigh and leaned in to nip at the enticing flesh of his earlobe. "Suits me."

THANK YOU!

Thank you for reading *Deuce*!

For two guys happy to stand up in public and do their thing, Garrett and Spencer proved to be quite shy souls. First, I had to figure out their secret door knock, and only then did they let me sneak a peek into their private world.

Perhaps I picked up some of Spencer's dogged determination along the way, because the challenge of discovering their story and getting it down on the page was all the sweeter for it.

If you'd like to encourage Spencer and Garrett to leave their door unlocked as they embark on their glorious journey into the future, please consider sharing your thoughts in a rating or review.

ele

Want to know what's happening next in Tennyson Bend?
Escape to *Thrall*, a tropical island adventure featuring grumpy Malone and sunshine Jet.

For quirky content and updates on future books, subscribe to my newsletter at https://ptambler.com/newsletter-sign-up/

ALSO BY PT AMBLER

Tennyson Bend:
Haven
Deuce
Thrall

—∞—

Duly Domesticated:
Where There's a Wil, There's a Way
I'll Make a Manny Out of You

—∞—

For an updated list, please visit:
ptambler.com/books

ABOUT PT AMBLER

PT Ambler is an Aussie MM romance author who gets a ridiculous amount of joy letting her guys run rampant on the page.

Other fun things include sing-along road trips, zoning out in nature, day dreaming, people-watching in cafes, and coffee...smooth, delicious coffee, covered in shavings of rich, dark chocolate...mmm.

One of these days, she's going to write a novel set in a café about a gorgeous barista, who... (PT drifts away into a caffeine-fuelled daydream).

To find out more, check out https://ptambler.com, sign up for my newsletter at https://ptambler.com/newsletter-sign-up/, or catch me (occasionally) on Instagram at https://www.instagram.com/pt_ambler/.